HITCHED: THE BACHELORETTE

G.K. DEROSA

Print ISBN: 9781798037751

Cover Designer: Sanja Gombar www.fantasybookcoverdesign.com

Published in 2019 by G.K. DeRosa LLC
Palm Beach, Florida
www.gkderosa.com

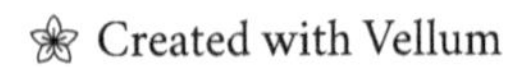

Thank you to all my fantastic fans!
~ G.K. DeRosa

CONTENTS

CHAPTER 1

The harsh white light of the camera burns my eyes. I blink rapidly to keep them from watering. Beads of sweat accumulate on my brow, but I'm too nervous to wipe them away. Now I know exactly how a deer feels, frozen under the glare of neon headlights. The red dot on the camera continues to blink at me, taunting. My heart beats out a frantic staccato as I clutch the pages in my lap. Every ounce of moisture has evaporated, and my tongue is stuck to the roof of my mouth.

"Ms. Starr, are you okay?" The casting director shoots me a narrowed glare. He and the associate producer stand in the shadow of the blinding light just to the right of the camera guy. Even in the shadows, I recognize the A.P., Tycen Vale. His trademark pinstripe suit reeks of wealth and power. He's a relative newcomer in the Hollywood scene according to Gianfranco, my agent, but he's young and whatever he touches turns to ratings gold.

I chew on my lower lip and clamp my hands together in my lap to keep them from shaking. *Get it together, Kimmie-Jayne*!

This is my biggest audition yet, and I'm totally about to blow it. Okay, so maybe I've only had three since moving to L.A. two months ago, but this is definitely the most important one.

"Did your agent not give you the sides?" Again the casting director levels me with his gaze, icy blue eyes freezing the dribble of sweat snaking down my back.

Ack! Why can't I remember his name? *So much for being prepared.*

I stare down at the short selection from the script that Gianfranco sent me, my pulse rapidly elevating. I did have it memorized a few hours ago, but every single word has leaked out of my brain at the moment. Why does a reality TV show need a script anyway?

The camera guy steps out from behind the mounted camcorder and gives me a smile. His warm grin is sweet and disarming, and the tension in my shoulders relents a tad. He runs his hand through his sandy-brown hair and regards me. "It might help if you pretend you're talking to me, instead of looking right into the camera lens."

I swallow thickly and nod, releasing the clenched sheet of paper in my hands. The casting director and the A.P. wear matching expressions of boredom, and I decide to turn my focus toward Camera Guy since he seems the nicest of the bunch. His gray Henley and distressed jeans give him a relaxed vibe, unlike the other two in their sleek tailored suits.

Voices filter through the walls of the casting office. They're so thin I can hear a feminine voice reciting the lines I was supposed to have memorized through the cheap plaster. I bet she's killing it. Unlike me.

I draw in a breath, and Camera Guy winks at me. Okay, I'm ready. "Hi, I'm Kimmie-Jayne, and I'm twenty years old from Clarksville, Missouri. I think I'd be the perfect choice for the starring role on *Hitched* because I'm ready for love. I've never dated much—only one guy actually. He was my high school sweetheart. Getting to know twenty-five guys all at once would be the perfect way to make up for my lack of experience and fast-forward the dating game." I glance up, and Tycen Vale is staring at his phone—probably texting someone. The casting director has his arms folded across his chest, and he's looking in my direction but his face is a blank mask. I'm totally bungling this. My shoulders sag, but I continue. "I'm looking for a guy that's sweet, smart and adventurous, but mostly someone that knows how to treat a girl like a lady. Basically I'm looking for my very own prince charming."

At that, Camera Guy smirks, and heat floods my cheeks.

"Okay, now from the script," says Icy Blues without even looking up. He ticks his head at Camera Guy. "Cross will read with you."

I squirm in my seat and cross my legs. I would never in a million years say any of these things on an actual date. Steeling my nerves, I begin, returning my gaze to Camera Guy—or Cross. "My last boyfriend was a terrible kisser. How would you describe your kissing style—an excited Golden Retriever, a cold trout or a sneaky boa?" I try not to cringe as I finish spouting out the terribly cheesy line. Who writes this stuff?

A laugh tumbles from Cross's lips as he scans the page he's holding. The casting director shoots him a glare and he clears his throat, his lips thinning. "Definitely a boa, baby. I'd wrap you in my arms and never let go. Then when you'd least expect it, I'd snake my tongue between your lips and slither around until your toes curl."

A peal of laughter explodes from my clenched teeth, and all eyes whip toward me. I quickly clap my hand over my mouth, but it's no use, I can't stop laughing. After the intensely building tension, I think I'm actually losing it. Plus that is the cheesiest line I've ever heard in my life.

Cross starts to chuckle, and even the A.P. and Icy Blue crack smiles.

"Do guys really say this stuff?" I can't help it; the words pop out of my mouth. "I thought this was supposed to be reality television."

"Only d-bags," says Cross, earning a pointed glare from the A.P. He shrugs and drops the sheet of paper on the desk. "What? It's true. Whoever writes this stuff needs to get out more."

Tycen's light brows draw together, fixing on Cross. "It's a good thing we don't pay you for your editorial critique." He ticks his head at the script thrown on the desk.

Cross grunts and picks it up again, flipping through a few pages, then turns to Icy Blue. "Where do you want me to start, Cullen?"

Yes—that's it! The casting director's name is Cullen Andrews. Gianfranco didn't know much about him.

"Page four, second line," he mutters.

I quickly flip through the pages in my head, hoping I remember my lines.

Cross clears his throat, and his warm hazel eyes meet mine. "I'm taking you out tonight, babe, and I *really* want to get to know you better. What would I have to do to seal the deal?"

His lip lifts in the corner, but I push down the bout of laughter threatening to bubble out and concentrate on the top of his head. The words flow smoothly for once. "A candlelight dinner on the beach followed by a moonlit walk along the sandy shore would do it for me, baby. I don't have a problem with sand in my pa—hair." Then I wink, and I'm sure I look ridiculous, but that's what the stage directions call for.

The associate producer lifts his hand, silencing Cross who's about to read the next line. Tycen's gaze rakes over me, like he's looking at me for the first time since I sat down. "That's it for now. We'll be in touch."

That's it? There are at least another two pages to get through. I try to mask the swell of disappointment and give him a smile as I reach for my purse on the floor.

"Oh, do you have a headshot with you?" asks Cullen, taking a step toward me.

No! Who uses those anymore? Gianfranco told me everything was digital these days. I quickly scramble through my tote bag, praying I have an old copy printed. My fingers close on a folded sheet of glossy paper, and I yank it out. It's crumpled, and there are coffee stains on the corner of the black and white photo. Dang it.

"That'll do," he says as he snatches it from my hand, his lips curling in disgust when they land on the brown stains.

My cheeks flush with embarrassment, and I swing my hair forward to hide behind the blonde curtain. Refusing to look up, I spin toward the door without even a goodbye.

Way to go, Kimmie.

I rush down the grimy stairs with my head down, pressing the script into my chest as tears prick my eyes. I need to be anywhere but here right now. How could I have ever thought I would make it in Los Angeles as an actress? I'm absolutely hopeless. Turning the corner, I nearly smack into a leggy blonde. I let out a yip of surprise, and the sheets of paper scatter all over the floor.

"Watch it!" The girl sneers at me as I crouch down to pick up the scattered pages, embarrassment squeezing my lungs. From the corner of my eye, I watch her saunter up the stairs, her red-soled Louboutins igniting another round of self-pity in my chest.

Maybe I should just give up now. With a huff, I shove the script into my tote bag and straighten, trying to gather the little dignity I have left. Heavier footsteps slap the concrete stairs above, and I race down the stairwell, hoping to avoid further embarrassment.

My luck it'll be one of the chosen bachelors, and he'll be super hot and I'll do something really stupid. Like open my mouth.

Finally reaching my beat-up Corolla in the parking lot, I sink into the worn cloth seat and exhale a long breath. Patting the peeling steering wheel, memories of the cross-country drive to L.A. fill my thoughts. No one thought my old girl would make the twenty-eight hour trek. "We proved them wrong, didn't we, Marilyn?" I named her after my all-time favorite actress, Marilyn Monroe, and I vowed to be as famous as she was one day.

I'll never forget the look on my parents' faces when I told them I was moving to Hollywood after finishing two years of community college. Times were tough, but with my parents help, I'd scraped up enough money to pay for my associate's degree and fund my trip to California afterward. Now I was worried Dad would never be able to retire from the Quik Mart because of it. I felt bad leaving, but I promised myself that when I made it big, I'd pay them back.

A smile splits my lips as the image of Becky Sue's slack-jawed expression flashes across my mind. My sister was so shocked at the news she almost dropped little Billy. She always has at least one kid strapped onto her while the other two pull at a leg or the hem of her skirt. That good-for-nothing husband of hers never spends more than a few minutes with those kids.

Sometimes I wonder if I wouldn't have wanted to leave home so badly if my sister's life hadn't turned out so crappy.

The ding of my phone tears me away from the musings into

my past. Digging it out of my purse, I grumble as the familiar name on the text message flashes across the screen. Bobby.

I miss you, Kimmie-Jayne.

I sigh and shove the phone back into my bag. Nope. I'm never going back. I refuse to become my mom or Becky Sue. I won't get trapped in Clarksville for the rest of my life with a crummy job and a crummier husband.

Not that Bobby is that bad. He was my first love—my first everything. When I found out he'd gotten a full ride to play baseball at the University of Missouri, I knew we were done. His path was set, predictable, and I wanted anything but. I want to be extraordinary. I want to be famous.

Maybe one day...

I flick the ignition, and Marilyn sputters to life. Turning out of the parking lot, I veer toward the sign for the freeway. I glance at the clock on the dash as I merge onto the on-ramp. Luckily, I have almost an hour until my shift starts. With this traffic, I'll just make it in time.

The fifty-five minute bumper-to-bumper drive passes slower than watching the corn grow on Uncle Jimmy's farm. When I finally pull into the parking lot, I'm exhausted. Or maybe just depressed. I squirm out of my cute audition sundress and into a bright yellow uniform shirt and black pants. Tugging the red apron out from under the passenger's seat, I grimace. Through the windshield, the stupid chicken on the obnoxious red and yellow sign stares down at me.

I grab a scrunchie from the center console and pull my blonde hair back, adjusting my red visor under my ponytail.

That's right. I work at a fast-food chicken joint.

CHAPTER 2

The best thing about working at a crappy fast food establishment is the free meals. Coming from Clarksville, Missouri, finding authentic Mexican food is a pretty impossible task. At least here, I get my belly's fill and it's not half bad.

Barreling through the front door, the scent of citrus, garlic and roasted meat fills my nostrils. My stomach rumbles, reminding me I haven't eaten all day. I'm totally having two orders of tacos for lunch. No reason to watch my weight after the blundered audition. The bell above the door chimes loudly, announcing my late arrival. I hastily throw the fire-engine-red apron over my head and tie it around my waist.

Hector stands by the cash register glaring, his chubby hands in tight fists on his hips. "*Ay chica*, you late again."

"I know. I'm so sorry, Hector. I just can't seem to get used to this traffic." I rush behind the counter, clock in, and slip my name badge on.

"Give her a break, *jefe*." Lupita saunters over to my side and gives me a good hip bump. With her petite frame and darting dark eyes, she's the only person that manages to look cute in our hideous uniforms. "She had an audition today. Our little *gringuita* is going to be a big star soon."

I give her a grateful smile as Hector grunts and trudges away. I would never survive working at Pollo Loco without her.

"So how did it go?" she asks as soon as the door to the back office slams shut.

"I totally blew it." I lean against the front counter and sigh. The place is empty. We're in that awkward time between breakfast and lunch so I can vent.

"*Ay, no mami,* I'm sure it wasn't that bad." She adjusts my nametag and looks up at me from under a curtain of dark lashes. Lashes that I'd kill for. Lupita is beautiful and exotic, and I'm just plain. A plain Jane. "What was it for again?"

"It's a new dating reality show called *Hitched.*" My voice goes up a notch, and even I can hear the excitement in my tone. I attempt to suppress it because there's no way I landed the role after that cringe-worthy audition. "It takes place on some remote island, and one girl gets picked to date twenty-five guys. At the end, she chooses one to marry."

Lupita's expressive eyes widen. "Seriously? You'd marry some random guy?"

I shrug. "My agent said most of it is fake, but what if I really do meet the one?"

She laughs and flicks my visor up. "You really are one of those hopeless romantics, aren't you, chica?" She takes a sip from her soda and points a hot-pink manicured fingernail at me. "You better be careful, Kimmie-Jayne, I'm worried for you. Hollywood is going to eat you up and spit you out. You gotta be tough if you want to survive in this city."

"I know," I mutter, folding my hands over my chest.

The jingle of chiming bells draws my attention to the door,

and a herd of teenagers make their way toward the counter. I glance at Lupita, and she rolls her eyes. Gossip time is over, and the lunch rush is about to begin.

I plaster a smile on my face and take a deep breath. "Welcome to Pollo Loco, what can I get you today?"

The next hour goes by in a rush of faces, piles of fire-grilled chicken, and overwhelming scents of cilantro and garlic. Every table in the small diner is filled, but the line has finally disappeared. I grab a drink from the soda fountain and lean against the counter, watching the customers scarf down their food.

My stomach rumbles again, reminding me I still haven't eaten. I glance at my watch. Fifteen more minutes until my lunch break.

Three police officers huddle around a table a few feet away from the counter. I can't help my gaze shifting in their direction. There's something so hot about a man in uniform. I move closer to get a better look at one of the guys. He looks about my age, maybe older, around early-twenties. His broad shoulders and sandy-blonde hair pique my interest.

"I'm telling you I saw one of them," says one of the other police officers.

Broad Shoulders lifts a brow. "A supernatural?"

The man nods, his lips tightly pressed together. "He was more beast than man. His hair was shaggy, and he had pointy fangs instead of teeth."

"You're full of it, Riley," says the third guy, chuckling.

He lifts his right hand up. "I swear on my mother's grave. The thing that attacked that woman in The Valley wasn't human. Come on, you guys. We've all heard the rumors. We aren't the only creatures in this world."

Broad Shoulders' gaze turns to me, and I quickly divert my eyes. Great first impression. The cute guy is going to think I was eavesdropping on their conversation.

He whispers something to the other two, and I can't make out another word of their discussion. I take a long gulp of soda as my mind plays back their exchange. Could there really be supernaturals living among us?

The police officer is right about the rumors. They've been running rampant for months. Growing up in small town, Missouri, I'd never heard a thing about the paranormal until I moved to L.A. I didn't believe it one bit.

A chill slithers down my spine as the gruesome images from the news flash across my mind. There were a whole string of animal attacks at Runyon Canyon in the Santa Monica Mountains. It is *the* place to go hiking—luckily, I'm too poor to live anywhere near there. I live with my horrible roommate in what I like to call Beverly Hills adjacent. Also known as The Valley.

"Are you okay? You're like ten times paler than normal." Lupita sneaks up behind me, and I almost pee myself.

I glance back at the group of police officers, but they seem to have changed topics. They're laughing and joking around now. "Yeah, it's nothing."

"Come on, chica. You look like you saw a ghost or something."

I pull her away from the counter to the grill, the scent of roasted chicken thick in the air clinging to my pores. Lowering my visor, I whisper, "Do you believe the rumors—about the supernaturals?"

She plants her hands on her curvy hips and arches a perfectly-tweezed brow. "Of course, I do, chica." Her hand flies to her forehead then her chest as she makes the sign of the cross. "My *abuelita* comes to visit me every year on Dia de Los Muertos. And I know spirits aren't the only paranormal things lurking around here." She lowers her voice and leans in. "You know that really pale guy that only comes in at night?"

I nod, knowing exactly whom she's talking about. There is something about that customer that always makes my skin crawl.

"The guys in the back think he's a vampire."

My eyes widen, and I'm sure I look like some crazed cartoon character. "There's no such thing as vampires," I hiss.

She shakes her head, clucking her tongue. "I don't know, but Ramos said he always asks for undercooked chicken."

Eww. I glance at the grill and the slabs of pink meat thrown across the fire.

The bell chimes, and my eyes turn toward the door—to a pair of warm hazel irises. *Oh shnikes*! I just can't get a break. I dive down behind the counter, praying the good-looking guy walking in doesn't see me.

"What's the matter with you, *loca*?" Lupita yanks on my ponytail as I crouch behind her.

"Kimmie-Jayne is that you?" says a smooth, deep voice.

Busted. I stay hidden, pulling the visor further over my face. Maybe he'll go away.

"Oye, chica, there's a hot guy here asking about you."

Traitor! I adjust my apron over my shirt and muster my last shred of dignity, forcing myself to stand.

Camera Guy smirks as I straighten to my full height and meet his gaze. He's actually cuter than he seemed in the dark audition room. Streaks of blonde run through his sandy-brown hair and coupled with his tan skin, he's giving off a total hot surfer vibe.

"I thought that was you," he says as he adjusts the sunglasses perched on his head.

"Yup. It's me," I mutter as heat floods my cheeks. What the heck is this guy doing all the way out in Sherman Oaks?

Lupita bumps her hip into mine and flashes a sexy smile.

"So Kimmie, when are you going to introduce me to your hottie friend?"

"Cristian Cross." He shoots her a big grin and extends his hand. "Kimmie and I only met today at her audition."

Lupita's dark brows nearly reach her hairline. "Oh! Wow, so are you some big shot producer?" She pouts out her full lower lip and gives him her hand.

He chuckles, and the sound is profound and soothing like hot cocoa on a wintry Missouri night. "No, nothing that important." He pries his hand from her tightly clenched fingers and rubs the back of his neck. "I'm the camera operator, and I do a little of the cinematography."

"It sure sounds important." Lupita leans over the counter, pressing her forearms against her chest giving Cross a clear view of her cleavage. It's her signature move. How she pulls off sexy in a bright yellow uniform shirt is beyond me.

Cross's gaze moves from her chest back to me. "Um… I'm actually glad I ran into you, Kimmie. Do you think you can take a break and eat lunch with me?"

My heart inches up my throat as I stare at him blankly.

"Kimmie!" Lupita's sharp elbow digs into my side, snapping me from a haze. "She'd love to have lunch with you. She was about to go on her break anyway."

I smile and nod at Cross as Lupita shoves me toward the employee locker room.

"Are you crazy?" I hiss as soon as we barrel through the swinging door, and we're out of earshot.

"Are you?" She squares off with me in front of the door. "That guy is one hot *tamale,* and you're going to let him get away?"

"But this is so embarrassing…" I pull the apron over my head, and the scent of onion and garlic fills my nostrils. "I reek of chicken."

"Who cares? If he likes you like this, it's saying a lot." She tugs the visor off my head and pulls my hair out of the tie, arranging the long blonde locks over my shoulders. "There—all set."

"Thank you."

She squeezes my hand and smacks my butt as I turn around. "Go get him, chica."

I can't help but laugh as I push through the doors into the main seating area. Cross sits at the corner table by the window and stands as soon as he sees me. "Sorry if I caught you off guard. If you have other plans for your break, I totally get it."

I glance down at the array of food on the table, and my stomach growls. "No, it's okay."

He pulls out my chair, and I almost die of shock. In my two months living in California, he is the first guy to perform the chivalrous gesture. "I asked the guy at the register what you liked so I took the liberty of ordering for you. I hope you don't mind."

Mind? My mouth is already salivating at the sight of the tacos. "Not at all. This is perfect, thanks."

I restrain myself from shoving the whole taco in my mouth and instead take a dainty bite in case he tries to talk to me. After the audition fiasco, I can't fathom why he'd ever want to see me again. And is it really a coincidence he ended up here?

He looks up at me over his burrito, his hazel eyes flitting over me. I quickly swallow the mouthful of chicken and take a sip of soda. "So…" he says, then a wicked smile splits his lips, "What do I have to do to seal the deal?"

A big laugh tumbles out, and I almost spit my drink out with it. Clapping my hand over my mouth, I pull myself together and make sure the beverage goes down my throat and not all over his face. "Is that really how guys talk on the show?"

I finally ask when I catch my breath. "Because if it is, then maybe it's a good thing I botched the audition."

He rolls his eyes. "Nah, don't say that. You did fine. And yeah, some of them do spout out lines like that, even without the prompting. To be honest, most of the interactions aren't that scripted, the writers just like to give the show a general direction. If there's enough drama without them, they tend to stay out of it."

"Ugh, I would give anything to be chosen for *Hitched*."

"Really?" His brows draw together, a slight frown crossing his handsome face. "Why would a beautiful girl like you need a TV show to find love? Or are you only doing it for the exposure?"

Heat seeps up my neck, and I'm surely as red as one of the tomatoes on my taco. I stare down at my plate and shrug. "A little of both I guess. I don't know. There's something romantic about the idea of it."

His hand suddenly finds mine across the table and warmth trickles into my fingers. "Listen, Kimmie-Jayne, you're too good for that show. There are some things you don't know and—"

A phone buzzes in his pocket cutting him off. He pulls it out and glances at the screen, his lips thinning. "Sorry, I gotta get this. It's from the studio."

"Sure, no problem."

I watch him as he walks away, fully appreciating his cute perky butt in those tight jeans. I laugh internally; I've been spending way too much time with Lupita.

The spicy scent of the tacos calls to me so I dig back in, scarfing the rest down before Cross gets back. From the corner of my eye, his pacing form draws my attention through the window. He's yelling at whoever is on the other side of the line and marching back and forth like a caged animal. I press my ear to the window, but the double-paned glass doesn't allow for a single syllable to be heard.

A minute later, he shoves the phone back into his pocket and heads back inside. I tear my gaze away from the window and suck down a big slurp of soda to wash down the tacos before he reaches the table.

"Sorry about that. It was Cullen, the casting director." Bright crimson flushes his cheeks, and he sounds like he just ran a marathon.

"Is everything okay?"

He opens his mouth then snaps it shut as if reconsidering just as my phone dings. I quickly silence the text message alert and glance back up at him.

"You should probably get that." He nods at my phone sticking out of my breast pocket.

My brows shoot up as I meet his troubled gaze. "How do you know who it is?" I assumed it was Bobby again and really didn't want to deal with him right now.

"Just a guess."

I pull my cell out and stare at the screen. It's a message from Gianfranco, my agent. Opening the messenger app, I scan the words once then twice as my pulse skyrockets. I have to read it again because I can't believe what I'm seeing.

Congratulations, bella. You are the new star of Hitched.

CHAPTER 3

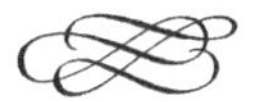

How is this happening? How did I score the starring role in one of the most talked about shows in Hollywood?

Okay so maybe that is a little of an exaggeration, but to me this is beyond huge.

The drive home that evening flies by in a blur as thousands of unanswered questions tumble around in my mind. I'm meeting with Gianfranco in the morning to go over all the specifics, and there is no way I'll be able to sleep a wink tonight. Behind all the excitement, a tiny dark cloud rains on my parade—Cross's odd reaction to the news.

Pulling into a spot in front of the old duplex, I shift Marilyn into park and draw in a breath. I really shouldn't care what the camera guy thinks, but I do. He almost seemed disappointed—worried even, and for the life of me, I can't understand why. I shake my head pushing the dark thoughts away. This is no time for moping; I should be breaking out the champagne. This could be it: my big break.

I need to call my parents—as much as I'm certain they

didn't think I'd ever really make it, I know they'll be happy for me. Unbuckling my seatbelt, I settle into my seat and dial their number. Mom answers on the second ring.

I don't even let her get a word in. "I got a starring role on a new TV show, Mom!"

"Oh, congratulations, Kimmie-Jayne. I'm so happy for you." But her voice doesn't sound happy at all.

"Is everything okay?"

She clears her throat, and it's only then I realize she's been crying.

"Mom, what is it? Is it Dad?"

"It's his blood pressure. You know how he is. He's stubborn and works too hard and... It went through the roof while he was at work today, and now he's in the hospital."

I suck in a sharp breath. "But he's going to be okay?"

"If he takes it easy. But you know that's like asking a dog not to bark."

"I'm sorry. I didn't realize things were so bad at home." A wave of guilt crashes over me for leaving them.

"It's not your fault. And please don't tell your father I told you. He was adamant that no one find out. Even Becky Sue doesn't know yet."

"Okay, I won't."

"I gotta run, honey. I don't want to miss visiting hours at the hospital. I'm hoping they'll let me bring him home tomorrow."

"Okay, keep me posted and tell Dad I love him."

"I will and congratulations on the job. You'll have to tell me more about it next time."

"Thanks, Mom." I tuck the phone back into my purse and exhale a long breath. He'll be fine. This job is exactly what I need to launch my career. Then I'll be able to take care of my parents, and Dad can finally retire.

Inserting the key into the lock of my front door, I hope Avery isn't home. No one could suck the excitement out of my news like she would. As a wannabe screenwriter, she looks down on all actors—especially me. A total snob, she's convinced she's going to be the next Scorsese. Just because she landed a job in the mailroom at WME Entertainment right out of college and met the legendary director once, doesn't mean she is better than me. To be honest, met is a strong word for their interaction. Mr. Scorsese passed by her in the hallway and apologized for bumping her arm. It barely counts in my opinion.

Avery peers over her glasses as I walk in, looking up from her laptop. She's got a pen sticking out of her messy bun and her *F—Off, I'm Writing* mug sits on the coffee table. Oh, did I forget to mention, she's writing the next blockbuster?

"You stink more than usual," she says, then lowers her gaze back to her computer.

I bite back the angry retort, knowing nothing could piss her off more than my news about landing the job. "It's a good thing I'll be putting in my notice tomorrow, then."

Her eyes jump back up to mine as I saunter to the couch. "You got another job?"

I nod, a huge grin plastered across my face. "An *acting* job—the starring role actually."

She sets her laptop down on the coffee table and pushes her glasses further up the bridge of her pixie nose. "For what?"

"Hitched."

"That new reality dating show?" She moves to the edge of the sofa, her eyes widening.

"Yup." I knew she'd know exactly what I was talking about. Working in the mailroom at one of the biggest talent agencies in the world does have its benefits. Not that I'd ever admit that to Avery.

She grunts and takes a sip from her mug. "No one at WME even understands why Sheppard Hawk took on that project. It's some no-name indie production company."

Sheppard Hawk is the executive producer and also the *it man* in Hollywood right now. Tycen Vale's his associate producer and right-hand man—and the guy I made a total fool of myself in front of at the audition.

"Well, I don't know why he took it and frankly, I don't care." As long as I got the job.

"When do you start? Where are they filming? How much are they paying you?" Avery starts peppering me with questions I haven't even had time to consider.

"I don't really know anything yet. I'm meeting with Gianfranco tomorrow." I slouch down on the couch, tucking my legs underneath me. It's times like these I wish I had my own room instead of sleeping on the pullout. Maybe after this big break, I'll have enough money to afford my own place.

A girl could dream.

"I'm surprised Gianfranco scored you that audition. Isn't his specialty porn?"

I nearly choke on my own spit. Gianfranco might not be a top tier agent like the ones at WME and he could be a little sketchy at times, but that is over the line. Okay so maybe he did bring up the option of erotic performances, but only one time, and he never did again once I told him it wasn't happening. Ever.

"Whatever," I hiss, jumping up and ducking into the bathroom. It is my only refuge in our small one-bedroom apartment. I light a few scented candles and turn on the faucet in the tub. The warm steam and soothing aromas fill the room, immediately calming my nerves.

This is so not how I should be celebrating landing my first starring role. First the news about Dad and then having to deal with Avery's snide comments. Where's the champagne and the "Congratulations, Kimmie-Jayne, you finally did it"? I huff and peel off my uniform, the odor of the grill and Latin spices seeping from my pores.

Stepping into the tub, the heated water is like a warm embrace. All I need now is a glass of wine, and I'd be happy. I mentally scold myself for not having thought of the wine before getting into the tub. Avery always has a few open bottles in the fridge, and I'd be a liar if I said I'd never snuck a glass here and there. It's still a few months until my twenty-first birthday, and I'm too broke to spring for a fake I.D. Closing my eyes and leaning my head back, I imagine what the twenty-five bachelors are going to be like. I can't help the ridiculous smile that sneaks up on me.

Twenty-five guys competing to date me? How did I get so lucky? How will I ever choose?

After the bath, I'm in much better spirits. Even Avery's resting-witch face doesn't get me down when I emerge from the bathroom. She's still sprawled across the couch, typing away. She won't even tell me what her stupid screenplay is about; she's paranoid I'll steal her idea. As if.

"Um, I'd like to get some sleep. I kind of have a big day tomorrow."

She rolls her eyes and turns the laptop toward me. It's opened to her WME email account. "I thought you'd like to know what people are saying about the show."

Chewing on my lower lip, I stare at her blankly. *Don't give in, Kimmie. She's just trying to get a rise out of you.*

"Or don't. Whatever." She shrugs and goes to close her Mac, but I slip my hand in, stopping her. An obnoxious smile splits her lips, but I ignore it.

I click on the conversation thread, already regretting it. The subject line says *Hitched – fab or flop?* It's from one of the executives at WME and apparently has made the rounds to practically every department in the agency.

"I'm going to bed." Avery takes her mug and heads toward the kitchen still wearing a smug smile. She turns back before disappearing around the corner. "Turn it off when you're done and don't snoop around the other emails, okay?"

"Fine," I mutter. Like I care about her stupid work correspondence. Scanning the fifty-plus emails in the thread, my eyes land on snippets of conversations.

"Sheppard is committing social suicide with this one."

"That twist is going to make that poor girl's head spin."

"Do you think the rumors are true?"

"There is definitely something weird going on with that production crew."

I slam the laptop shut, not wanting to read another word as hot tears pool in my eyes. It's only gossip. People are jealous and say mean things, especially in Hollywood. I throw the large cushions on the floor and heave out the pullout bed. Sleep—I just need a good night of sleep and tomorrow Gianfranco will explain everything.

I flop down on the bed and pull the comforter up to my chin. Closing my eyes, I try to still my racing thoughts, but it's no use. I'm as keyed up as a newly strung guitar. What if this is all a huge mistake?

CHAPTER 4

"Ciao, bella!" Gianfranco's musky cologne hits me as his office door swings open. The odor of his peppery perfume is almost as thick as his Italian accent. He wraps me in a warm embrace, kissing both of my cheeks, making me blush. I didn't think I'd ever get used to his overly affectionate Italian ways.

The Starkowskis were not huggers. I could probably count the number of times my mom or dad hugged me on two hands. Oh, that's right, Starkowski is my real last name. Starr is my stage name. It was Gianfranco's idea, and I couldn't really argue. How many celebrities do you know of with the last name Starkowski? None. I can tell you.

"Come, sit." Gianfranco ushers me into his tiny office. I have to tuck my chair in all the way under his desk before he can even close the door. His salt and pepper hair is neatly gelled back, his light blue button down shirt impeccable and even buttoned up most of the way for a change. He ducks down behind his desk and pops up with a bottle of champagne.

"Today we celebrate, bella." A huge grin takes up most of his face, and his happiness is contagious.

A laugh tumbles out of my mouth as he pops the cork and pours the bubbly liquid into two flutes. It doesn't even matter that they're plastic or that the champagne is Cook's. He's the first person to be genuinely excited for me.

"Thank you, Gianfranco." I lift my glass to his and offer him my best smile. "I would've never made it this far without you."

He winks as he takes a sip. "I knew you were a star, Kimmie-Jayne. From the first time I saw you I said to myself, Gianfranco, *hai trovato una stella*—you've found your star."

Stella—a star. Could it really be true? Little Kimmie-Jayne Starkowski, the next big thing in Hollywood? My heart thumps louder as I take a big gulp of champagne. The fizzy bubbles go straight to my head and warmth fills my chest. Now this is the type of celebration I was envisioning.

"So what happens now?"

"Now, we go to meet the producers and director. We discuss the terms, and you sign the papers." He stands and grabs his designer jacket from the back of his worn leather chair. I've never understood how Gianfranco could afford his fancy suits and still have such a crappy office.

I follow his lead and get to my feet as excitement thrums in my veins. "I have so many questions; I don't even know where to begin."

"Don't worry, bella. They will answer everything when we get there."

"Where exactly are we going?" I ask as I throw my tote over my shoulder. The seedy building in Burbank where I auditioned fills my vision.

"To the Warner Brothers lot."

"What?" I'm pretty sure my eyes are going to pop out of my head.

"We go to Sheppard Hawk's office, stella mia."

Eeek! Wait until Avery hears I went to Warner Brothers. I wonder how many celebs I'll see on the way.

"*Andiamo*." Gianfranco leads me out of his office as my mind swirls in disbelief.

This is it. This is really happening.

GIANFRANCO PULLS his sporty Alfa Romeo up to the guard gate, and I'm fairly certain my heart is going to explode out of my chest. The iconic Warner Brothers water tower peers over us, soaring above the soundstages sprawled across the lot. I don't even hear what Gianfranco tells the guard over the erratic jackhammering of my heart, but moments later we're driving through the gate.

We head to the left, past a few soundstages and park in front of a cluster of beige mid-rise buildings. As we walk to the entrance, I grip my tote bag so tightly, I nearly lose feeling in my fingers. The elevator ride to the top floor is a blur as are the people passing me in the hallway. Leonardo di Caprio could have walked right by me, and I wouldn't have realized it.

"Relax, bella." Gianfranco places his hand on the small of my back, and as much as the intimate gesture would normally have disturbed me, today I find it comforting.

A cute blonde admin greets us at the front desk and ushers us to the waiting area. "Mr. Hawk will be right with you."

I force myself to smile and nod, then sit on the pristine white leather couch. The over-sized flat-screen TV across from me is set on E!, and it's recapping the Golden Globe nominations. I'm at the edge of my seat, my knee bouncing uncontrollably. My stomach is doing somersaults, and I wipe my sweaty palms on my sundress.

Gianfranco chuckles. "Bella, you already got the part. There is no need to be so nervous."

I guess that's what I'm having a hard time believing—that I'd actually gotten it. How in the world did that happen? I keep thinking they're going to realize they've made a terrible mistake.

The blonde rushes back in minutes later, a tablet pressed against her sleek black dress. "I'm sorry, but there's been a change of plans."

My heart plummets, taking my stomach along with it. It's like I'm on the breakaway of a runaway rollercoaster. Here it is —they made a mistake—they don't want me.

"What do you mean?" asks Gianfranco.

I'm still struggling to get my lungs to start working again so speech is out of the question.

"Mr. Hawk and Mr. Dax have decided to move up the production schedule. Ms. Starr will have to fill out the paperwork in the jet on the way."

"The jet?" I squeak.

She nods, pulling me to my feet. "Come, come. You can get a ride to the private airport with some of the crew. They're leaving now." She turns to Gianfranco. "Someone will be in touch with you to sort out all the details later."

My mouth hangs open as my gaze bounces back and forth between the admin and my agent.

Gianfranco lifts a shoulder and gives me a reassuring smile. "*Bene*. Don't worry, bella. I leave you in good hands."

That's it? He's just going to leave me?

"But I don't have any clothes… my toothbrush, hair brush, anything." I scramble to get the words out as the blonde shuffles me toward the exit, and Gianfranco obediently follows behind.

"Don't worry, everything will be provided when you arrive on location."

"And where is that exactly?"

Her light brows furrow as she scans the tablet. "It's a surprise, apparently."

I swallow trying to create some moisture in my mouth. It's as dry as the desert in Palm Springs.

The front doors glide open, and a charter bus idles by the sidewalk. A few men hustle around it, loading it with bulky black bags of what I assume is production equipment. The admin points at the huge vehicle. "Here's your ride."

The bus door opens and a familiar face peeks out, quelling the rising terror.

"Ms. Starr, nice to see you again." Cross gives me a tight-lipped smile, and all the warmth in his voice from yesterday is gone. His tone is professional and nothing more.

"Nice to see you, too," I manage.

"Do you have any luggage to load in?"

I shake my head. "No. This was all a bit unexpected."

The admin tears her gaze away from the tablet to glance up at Cross. "Change of plans. She's riding with you guys. Mr. Hawk wants to start filming right away."

"I see." He rubs his chin, and then crosses his arms over his chest still regarding me.

"Okay, I go now, bella." Gianfranco interrupts the weird stare-off going on with Cross and gives me a big hug. "You will be wonderful. I know it, *piccola stella*."

"Thank you." I squeeze him hard for some inexplicable reason. When he pulls away, I find myself not wanting to let go. *Get it together, Kimmie*. This is what you've always wanted.

I finally release him and back away, clutching my tote to my chest. Gianfranco disappears around the bus, and small hands are shoving me up the steps of the ginormous vehicle.

Cross extends his hand and I take it, desperate for any sort of safety net in this whirlwind of chaos.

Less than half of the seats on the bus are occupied, but all eyes turn to me as I shimmy down the aisle.

"Everyone, this is Kimmie-Jayne Starr, *Hitched*'s new leading lady." Cross's voice thunders through the small space, and heat flushes my cheeks. A round of applause fills the bus, and I'm sure I'm fifty shades of red now.

"Thanks," I muster, and my voice is a few octaves higher than normal.

"Well, don't be shy, guys. Introduce yourselves."

People smile and wave and say their names and occupations, but every single one goes in one ear and out the other. I cringe, realizing I'll be spending the next few weeks of my life with these people, and I've already forgotten their names. Then it hits me I don't even know how long I'll be gone for.

"How long is filming?" I ask Cross as I take a seat halfway down the aisle.

He sits across the row from me, and the crease between his brows deepens. "Wow, they really didn't tell you anything, did they?"

"Nope. I thought I was going in to sign some papers and before I knew it, I was whisked onto the bus."

"Probably six to eight weeks—assuming everything goes well."

Two months? Well, Avery will be thrilled. I pull out my phone and shoot her a quick text. She may not like me very much, but I don't want her to think I've been kidnapped or murdered. While I'm at it, I send a quick message to Lupita, too. At least she'll be happy for me. I resolve to call my parents once we land to check in on Dad.

I glance over at Cross who's still watching me. A jumble of questions roll around in my mind, but I'm too much of a chicken to voice them. Most importantly, I want to know why he seemed upset that I'd gotten the job.

Instead, I opt for an easier subject. "Have you ever worked on a show like this before?"

He nods, his hazel eyes darkening. "Dax, the director, and I go way back. I've shot a few of his projects before."

That's interesting. Gianfranco didn't know much about Dax, and my googling hadn't unearthed anything on him either.

"Is he nice?" I'd heard some horror stories about Hollywood directors.

"Yeah, he's a good guy. Peculiar, like all geniuses." His lips twitch, and a glimpse of the guy I'd eaten with yesterday emerges.

"I'm super nervous about this, and I could really use a friend on set." The words pop out of my mouth before I can stop them. I may not have dated much, but even I should know telling a guy you want to be their friend is a stupid move.

He schools his expression into a smile. "I'll try, Kimmie, but we're not really supposed to interact with the talent."

My head spins so fast I'm fairly sure I'll have whiplash tomorrow. "The talent?"

"The crew is forbidden from developing relationships—friendship or otherwise, with you or any of the contestants. The whole idea of a reality TV show is to forget you're being filmed. It's easier to draw the line from the beginning and pretend the crew isn't even there."

An inexplicable pang shoots through my heart. The idea of not being able to talk to Cross saddens me in a way I hadn't expected. What he said makes sense, but still it seems unfair.

"I'm sorry to hear that. I like talking to you."

He grins, and it actually reaches his eyes this time. "I like talking to you too, Kimmie."

The bus slows and I slide forward, hitting the seat in front of me. I glance out the window at the shiny jet poised on the runway.

Cross stands, throwing a duffel bag over his shoulder. "You ready, Ms. Starr?"

I gulp and force my butt out of the seat. "As ready as I'll ever be."

CHAPTER 5

The rumble of the aircraft drowns out the wild beating of my heart as I step onto the retractable steps, clutching my purse like it's a lifejacket and I'm about to plunge into icy waters. Cross walks just behind me, his presence oddly comforting.

I step inside the swanky main cabin, and a flight attendant greets me with a megawatt smile. "Welcome, let me show you to your seat."

I nod and follow without speaking because I'm too busy checking out the lavishly appointed cabin. Pristine captain's chairs line both sides of the jet with mahogany tables and gold embellishments. The flight attendant escorts me to an empty seat which faces another unoccupied seat across from it. Two bubbling champagne flutes adorn the compact table in between.

A breath of relief escapes my clenched lips when Cross sits in the empty spot across from me. Tucking my bag underneath the roomy seat, I glance around the cabin as the rest of the crew gets situated. I still haven't seen anyone I recognize from the audition—thankfully.

"Do you guys always travel like this?" I ask Cross who's staring at his phone.

"Yeah, most of the time. Commercial jets don't generally fly to the locations we shoot at."

Hmm. They must be pretty remote sites then. It's not like LAX is some podunk little airport. I thought you could get anywhere in the world from there.

The crackle of the intercom puts an end to our short conversation. The captain introduces himself and informs us we'll be departing in a few minutes with a five hour estimated flight time.

Anxiety bubbles up inside me, a swirl of excitement and apprehension building. Where is this mysterious location?

Footsteps clattering up the metal stairs draw my attention to the door. A purple head of spiky hair pokes into the main cabin, and all the chatter immediately stops. The man props his aviator sunglasses on his head and scans the room, his darting gaze landing on me. Pale lavender irises rake over me, and a satisfied grin settles over his face. "Oh yeah, she'll do just fine."

I tear my gaze away from his to the three other men boarding the plane behind him. Icy blue eyes meet mine, and I cringe. Cullen, the casting director, steers Purple Hair toward me.

The other two men in fancy suits follow behind, all making a beeline straight toward me.

Cullen nods at Cross as he passes then settles his chilling gaze on me. "Dax, this is Kimmie-Jayne Starr."

I jump to my feet as soon as I recognize the name. So this is the mysterious director, Dax. He's younger than I'd imagined—early thirties at most and with a tall, lanky frame and a silver hoop dangling from the top of his ear. Sharp, high cheekbones give him an Asian vibe, but I can't stop staring at his eyes. Besides the slanted, feline shape, the light violet color is like none I've ever seen on a human before. The lilac hue is almost an exact replica of the fragrant lavender fields in Missouri.

Finally, I stop gawking and extend my hand, remembering my manners. "I'm so pleased to meet you, Mr. Dax."

He winks, and I swear deep lilac light pulsates from his irises. "Just call me, Dax, sweetheart. You can keep the formal titles for these two." He jerks his thumb over his shoulder, and I realize the man standing beside Tycen Vale must be the executive producer.

"Sheppard Hawk." The producer tucks his phone into the pocket of his pristine navy jacket and extends a hand. "I apologize for the rush, but there were some unforeseen circumstances that moved up our shooting timetable."

He squeezes my hand, and I'm surprised by the strength of his grip. He doesn't look like a guy who spends much time at the gym. With his portly physique, and fine salt and pepper hair, I picture him at a fancy gentleman's club smoking a big fat cigar and sipping cognac.

"It is such an honor to meet you, sir. You are truly a legend. I can't thank you enough for the opportunity."

"You can thank me by making *Hitched* a huge success."

I gulp. *No pressure.*

Sheppard turns to his associate producer. "And you've met Tycen, here."

"Yes, of course. Nice to see you again." I grab hold of his hand with both of mine. "Thank you so much for choosing me."

He tips his head toward Dax. "I'm afraid that honor goes to our director. Your audition tape had him from the get go."

Thank goodness he wasn't at the actual audition.

Dax flashes me a smile, those lilac eyes mesmerizing. "I can spot talent from a mile away."

"Thank you, then. I promise you won't regret your choice. I'll work harder than anyone and do whatever it takes to make this show a success."

From the corner of my eye, I catch Cross's expression darken, his lips twisting. I focus back on the men standing in front of me. Whatever Cross's problem is, I can't let it get to me.

Tycen pulls a stack of papers out of his briefcase and sets it on the table in front of me. "Here are all the contracts and non-disclosure agreements, etcetera. If you have any questions, ask Cross. He's pretty good with this stuff. Usually you'd be signing this with your agent and our in-house council, but it's all pretty standard."

"Sure, thanks."

"Enjoy the flight, Ms. Starr," says Sheppard, "we'll see you when we land." He, Tycen, and Dax disappear behind a door at the back of the plane.

Cullen nods a quick goodbye and moves toward the exit, and the flight attendant locks the cabin door behind him. I guess the casting director won't be joining us to this mysterious location. I can't say I'm sorry about that.

Picking up the thick booklets splayed across the table, I flip through a few pages. I can't believe this is really happening; it's all been such a whirlwind that I haven't had a second to process. My eyes land on the section on compensation and my eyes widen as I stare at all the zeros. This can't be right. My throat goes dry as I contemplate all the things I could do with that amount of money. I could finally afford my own place, and I'd have more than enough extra to send to my parents. Maybe Dad could finally retire from the Quik Mart. The possibilities are endless with this kind of money.

I scan the remaining pages, my mind still reeling with the exorbitant amount of money at my fingertips. Once I sign the contract, it'll be official. I'll be spending the next two months of my life dating twenty-five men. And at the end of that I could be engaged.

I suck in a sharp breath. I'm not sure what I'm more scared of, finding the one and committing or the heartbreak of discovering none of them are right for me. Or maybe I shouldn't even be thinking like that at all. It's just an acting gig —one that will propel me to fame and pay me a fortune.

"Don't forget to breathe, Kimmie."

I glance up to find Cross regarding me. His expression is hard to read—a mix of sympathy and regret? "Why aren't you happy about me getting this job?" The words are out of my mouth before I can stop them. I kind of have a problem keeping my thoughts to myself. I know I shouldn't care what he thinks, but I do.

His lips twist into a rueful smile. "That's not it at all, Kimmie." He leans forward and lowers his voice. I find myself doing the same thing so that our noses are only a few inches apart. "I *am* happy you got the role." He pauses and draws in a breath as his fingers creep toward mine. "I'm just not thrilled about the idea of having to share you with twenty-five other guys." He winks and I get the feeling he's making light of the comment, but his eyes are confessing something else.

My breath hitches as his gaze travels to my mouth. Unbidden, my tongue sweeps over my bottom lip, and I can't help but wonder what Cross's lips would feel like against mine.

The back door where the executive crew had disappeared whips open, smacking against the adjacent wall. Cross jumps back so quickly it's as if he's been thrown back against the seat. "Cross." Tycen fills the doorway, a scowl marring his handsome face. "Join us, would you?"

Cross clears his throat and rakes his hand through his sandy-brown hair. "Be right there."

I sit back in my seat, and the swarm of butterflies in my stomach settles. I force my gaze to the window instead of watching Cross fumble around with the briefcase under his chair. He's bent over, giving me a front row view of his firm behind. Squeezing my eyes shut, I mentally curse myself for the naughty thoughts floating through my mind.

"See you in a bit," he mutters.

I reopen my eyes and finally meet his gaze. If Tycen hadn't interrupted, would he have kissed me? No, he couldn't have. He just told me it was forbidden. Did I want him to? I push the thoughts away and give him a smile. I'm about to meet twenty-five eligible bachelors; this is no time to be developing feelings for someone. I pretend not to notice the yearning look in his eye and refocus on the paperwork in front of me. "See ya," I finally say with a wave.

At some point after signing and initialing dozens of pages, I must fall asleep because I awake to a strange blue light bathing the cabin. Rubbing my eyes, I shake the grogginess away to confirm what I'm seeing. A brilliant blue glow coats every inch of the sumptuous cabin including the passengers, but no one else seems to notice. Most of the crew is asleep, but a few people continue their low chatter oblivious to the eerie radiance crawling over them.

Am I the only one seeing this? And where's Cross? I search the cabin, but he's nowhere in sight.

A bout of turbulence knocks me around in my seat and I clutch the armrests, squeezing my eyes shut. When I reopen them, the light is gone.

What the heck?

I spin around in my chair, looking at the crew's reactions but no one even flinches. Am I going crazy now?

My stomach drops, alerting me of our descent before the captain's voice crackles to life on the speaker.

"Please return to your seats and fasten your seatbelts in preparation for landing. We'll be arriving in fifteen minutes. Thank you."

I push my window shade up, and my jaw drops. The scene below looks like something straight from a post card. A brilliant aqua ocean encircles a verdant mountainous chain of islands. Nothing but clear blue seas stretch out for miles. It's absolutely breathtaking.

Moments later, the wheels hit the ground, and my body lurches forward as the jet races down the runway. Through the small window, I catch a glimpse of lush green trees rushing by in a blur.

My pulse spikes, excitement free-flowing in my veins. This is it.

CHAPTER 6

A wave of sultry heat washes over me as I step off the airplane. The intoxicating scent of gardenias swirls in the air, tantalizing my nostrils. I can't take it all in fast enough. A lush tropical jungle stretches out before me, the narrow strip of cement runway encroaching in the vast canopy of green.

"This is beautiful," I mutter to myself.

Beyond the copse of trees, the brilliant turquoise waters lap lazily along the shore.

"Welcome to paradise." Cross's warm breath tickles my ear as he materializes behind me. Nudging me forward, he ushers me down the steps toward the line of golf carts that waits beside the runway. The rest of the crew piles into the electric vehicles, and none of them appear to be as taken by the exquisite scenery as I am.

Behind me, Dax and the producers emerge from the jet and walk past us toward the carts. Dax whirls around, tips his sunglasses forward and winks at me over his shoulder.

I shoot him a smile back, hoping my cheeks aren't flaming. I'm not used to that much attention from the opposite sex. I will have to get the blushing under control if I hope to survive the next few weeks.

"Come on," says Cross, placing his hand on the small of my back. "Jump on. This is our ride to the manor."

I follow him to the lead car and smile at the driver as I scoot in the back seat. He's a little guy, probably a few inches shorter than me. He tips his white cap and gives me a big toothy grin. My eyes land on his arms, drawn by the tattooed olive-green vines that climb up and down his forearms.

"Welcome to Mystic Cove, Miss Starr."

"Thank you. I'm really excited to be here. Where exactly is here by the way?"

The driver exchanges a quick glance with Cross over his shoulder. My companion squirms in the seat beside me before meeting my eyes. "We're on a small island chain in the South Pacific."

"Oh. Like Tahiti?"

"Something like that. It's privately owned—you won't find it on any map."

"Oh yeah, by who?" Owning an island like this has to cost millions.

"The production company, I believe."

"Okay." I turn my gaze to the lush jungle surroundings as the driver weaves through the dirt path. Exotic flowers in vivid pinks and purples dot the deep green bushes and vines. Fragrant scents swim in the air, finer than any perfume I've ever smelled.

I draw in a breath, taking it all in. Before long the dense foliage gives way to the sandy shoreline. The sound of crashing waves fills me with a sense of calm I haven't felt since leaving home months ago.

"There it is—Mystic Manor." The driver points a heavily tattooed arm as we turn a bend along the coastline.

My jaw unlocks, and I'm fairly certain someone's going to have to scrape it off the sandy beach. A sprawling mansion sits atop a rolling hill surrounded by acres of perfectly manicured land.

Cross leans over and lifts my chin, giving me a lop-sided smile. "Careful, you don't want to let the bugs in. There are all kinds of nasty ones out here in the jungle."

I swallow, unable to tear my eyes away from the immense wrought-iron gate we are quickly approaching. A beefy guy steps out of the guardhouse, dressed in all black, and tips his cap as we pull up.

"Welcome to Mystic Manor, Miss Starr."

Stamped across his golden nametag is the name Warrick. It suddenly occurs to me that our driver must be wearing one too, but I hadn't noticed it since I'd been so entranced by our surroundings.

"Thank you, Warrick," I say as the colossal gate creaks open.

The cart whizzes up the stone driveway, which is at least half a mile long. We pass tennis, basketball and volleyball courts, and an Olympic-sized pool complete with a bathhouse, and that's only the front part of the property. The turquoise ocean shimmers behind the impeccable Mediterranean-style mansion, and I can only imagine what the views must be like on the inside.

At the far end of the compound, sits another building with two floors of what look like apartments.

"That's where the crew lives," says Cross following my gaze. "It's not quite as luxurious as where you'll be staying."

We pull up to the circular driveway, and a gorgeous fountain with a marble angel in the center sprinkles me with water. The cool spritz feels amazing against my heated skin.

"This place is incredible..." My head swivels back and forth trying to take it all in as I descend the vehicle.

"See you soon, Miss."

I turn back to the driver and search his white uniform for a nametag. The gold badge glistens in the sunlight. "Thanks for the ride, Memmo." I wave, and he rewards me with a warm grin.

Cross leads me up the steps between two massive columns, and my heart rate picks up. The lavish mahogany double doors open, revealing a man and woman in matching gray uniforms. We walk through the arched entryway and stunning ocean views makeup the back wall of the foyer.

"Miss Starr, I presume," says the older man, dipping his head.

"Welcome home." The woman steps forward and curtsies.

Am I supposed to curtsy too? My knees wobble, and I'm terrified I'm going to fall flat on my face. I begin to bend a knee, but Cross shakes his head subtly and lifts me back up.

"Thank you," I mutter to the man and woman.

"This is Auriela and Faustus." Cross motions to each of them. "They're in charge of the house and staff."

"If you would like anything, you need only ask, Miss Starr." Auriela wears a kind smile, immediately setting my keyed-up nerves at ease. She reminds me of Mary Poppins only a few decades older.

"Please call me Kimmie-Jayne. We'll be spending quite some time together so there's no need for formality." The idea of having servants is simultaneously terrifying and intriguing. I never imagined anything like this in my wildest dreams.

Excited chatter draws my attention to the doorway, where another man and woman walk in, each carrying black bags and cases. These two are much younger than Auriela and Faustus—not to mention the guy has a mohawk with bright blue tips, and hot pink streaks highlight the girl's short white-blonde hair.

"Ohmygod, I cannot wait to get my hands on your hair!" The petite blonde rushes over, dropping her equipment across the long entryway, and squeezes my hands. Her dainty little fingers are running through my hair before I can open my mouth.

She circles me excitedly, bouncing around on her tiptoes. She reminds me of Tinkerbell on a caffeine high. I half expect translucent shimmery wings to sprout from her back at any moment.

Blue Mohawk steps forward, swatting her hands away. "Easy, Trix, she only just arrived. Give the girl a second to get comfortable." He leans in and kisses both of my cheeks as I stand there frozen. "Don't worry, little bug, we'll take good care of you. I'm Bash and this is Trixie. We're your personal stylists."

Trixie with a pixie cut. I can't help but laugh internally. Or maybe I'm losing my mind. How can any of this be real?

I'm still staring like a deer in headlights so Trixie and Bash take the lead. Each grabs an arm and steers me toward a grand spiral staircase off the main entryway.

"Do you two know where you're going?" shouts Cross.

"Don't worry, Cristian, we'll find it," Trixie calls over her shoulder.

"You have one hour till they get here."

"We know, we know." Bash tugs me up the stairs.

I pause to catch my breath on the landing and turn to Bash. "One hour until who gets here?"

"Why, the eligible bachelors of course." Trixie smiles from ear to ear, her words flowing like a melodic tune.

My heart jumps up my throat, and the beginnings of a full-blown panic attack tighten my chest. "Are you serious? Filming starts in one hour? I just got here, and I don't even have anything to wear."

They both nod, shooting me reassuring glances. "Don't worry, little bug, we'll have you camera-ready in no time."

I take the rest of the steps two at a time, my thundering heartbeats not from the uphill climb but from the anxiety spilling through my veins. This is really happening. Twenty-five guys are on their way to meet, date and possibly marry me.

We finally reach the top of the stairs, and a huge entertainment area sprawls before us. The biggest TV I've seen in my life hangs on the wall, and a bunch of comfy couches are situated around it. Two arched doorways sit on opposite sides of the open room, and Trixie leads the way toward the one on the right.

"This is your wing of the manor. The guys will be on that one." She points across the room. I sneak a peek, curious to see where they'll be staying, but I can't make anything out from this distance besides a long corridor.

"Don't worry, you'll get plenty of time to explore that part of the manor in the days to come." Bash winks, and heat floods my cheeks.

I hadn't even had time to think about the physical aspect of dating twenty-five guys. I'm not sure I can *kiss* more than one guy at a time let alone do other things with them. And with a show like this, I can only imagine what the producers expect.

Trixie tugs at my hand, pulling me down the hall toward my new living quarters. We pass a sitting area, a decent-sized kitchen, a large bedroom and another entertainment area before we reach the master bedroom. It's like an entire house within a house.

Bash throws open the French doors, and my hand claps over my mouth to keep my jaw from hitting the plush carpeting. We walk beneath a sparkling chandelier toward a massive canopied bed. It looks like it was plucked straight out of a fairy tale with delicate pink lace adornments.

The room is gigantic with a wrap-around balcony showcasing shimmering turquoise water below. Light grays and pinks give the room a modern but warm feel, and the tropical paintings on the walls add to the island vibe.

I don't think I'll ever want to leave.

I jump on the bed, stretching out and running my fingers over the soft comforter. It feels like I'm floating on a cloud.

"Hate to ruin your fun, Kimmie, but we've got a tight schedule." Trixie opens a pair of double doors on the other side of the room, revealing a closet big enough to hold my childhood bedroom.

I stumble across the room to get a closer look at the fully stocked wardrobe. "Holy shnike's." My hand runs along the fine fabrics of more dresses than they have in the women's department at Macy's.

Bash chuckles. "Did you just say Nike's? I don't think you'll find any of those in there."

"Nope, *shnike's*. I guess it does rhyme with Nike's. Something we used to say back home."

"Oh, you small town folk are so cute." Bash pinches my cheek—something I used to hate as a child, but coming from him is kind of endearing.

"I'm thinking this for the opening sequence." Trixie's got her slender fingers on the long skirt of a ball gown I've only seen the likes of on the red carpet at the Oscar's. On TV, of course. She pushes back the other dresses and hangs it on the tip of her finger, twirling it. The red sequins catch the light from the chandelier hanging overhead and the shimmery fabric comes alive with sparkles.

"Oh yes, definitely that one," says Bash.

"But it's so see-through..." I step closer and run my finger over the sheer bodice, lace embroidery and sequins strategically placed to cover the important parts. The rest of the sweeping gown flows to the floor with a trailing skirt. At least the bottom part isn't translucent. "I don't know about this."

"Little bug, you're going to have to toughen up if you want to survive this thing." He shoves the dress in my arms and hastens me toward the bathroom. "Go change."

I take a second to gawk at the marble Roman tub, vowing to enjoy a candle-lit bubble bath when this is all over. The bathroom is even bigger than the closet with marble and gold-encrusted everything. I quickly slip out of my sundress and step into the deep red gown. After a few unsuccessful attempts at zipping up the back, I give up and call for Trixie.

"Eeep!" Her petite hands fly to her mouth. "I was right. It's perfect for you." She zips me up in a flash, and I turn to my reflection in the mirror.

My breath hitches. The gown is beyond exquisite, hugging curves I didn't know I had. Surprisingly, the red lace and sequins cover my boobs perfectly, and with the high collar and long translucent sleeves I don't look half as scandalous as I'd imagined.

Trixie pulls my hair up off my shoulders and twists it on top of my head. "Definitely an up-do for tonight."

I nod because she's the professional after all.

She opens the bathroom door and shouts for Bash. "You have to come see this."

He saunters in lugging equipment, and his full lips form a capital O. Clapping his hands, his dark chocolate irises rake over me. "Oh honey, you are going to give those boys heart failure."

I shoot him an appreciative smile. "Thanks. I just hope they like me."

"What's there not to like?" He twirls me around, and the flowing skirt dances off the marble floor. "Okay, you're gorgeous. Now strip, so you can shower and then we can start with hair and makeup."

My eyes bulge out a bit as he crosses his arms over his chest.

"Little bug, you ain't got nothing I haven't seen before, and you definitely don't have anything I want. If you know what I mean."

I relax a shred and turn my back to Trixie so she can unzip me as Bash begins to unload more beauty products than I've ever seen in my life. She hands me a silky robe and positions a chair in front of the mirror. "Let's do this."

CHAPTER 7

Two quick knocks at the door send my heart aflutter. It flip-flops in my chest as I force my brain to string words together. "Come in."

Tycen and Dax saunter in, and I suddenly wish my stylists had stayed to keep me company. I am pretty sure Tycen hates me, and Dax… Well, I'm not certain what to make of him yet. His enigmatic purple irises scour over me for an intense moment until his lips twist into a grin. "Perfect," he growls.

Tycen hands me a few sheets of paper messily clipped together. "There's not much to the opening scene, but the writers want you to get an idea of what we're looking for."

I scan the first page, reading over the cheesy dialog and cringe. I'm so *not* using any of these ridiculous lines. When I finish, I glance up at Tycen. "I'm confused. If this is a reality show, why is there a script?"

"It's called scripted reality, sweetheart," answers Dax. "We want to make sure we keep it interesting. If you and the boys can prove capable of doing that on your own, the writers will back off."

"I see." I'd really like to meet these writers and give them a piece of my mind. I chew on my bottom lip. I have so many questions, and I'm not sure I'll ever get answers, but there is one in particular that's burning my tongue. "Is any of it real? I mean, my relationship with the guys. Will I really be engaged at the end of the show?"

Tycen and Dax exchange a glance, and the corner of Dax's lip curls up. "It's whatever you make of it, sweetheart."

The A.P. adjusts his tie and clears his throat. "What we care about are ratings, Kimmie-Jayne. If you happen to find the one, great, but we're not making any promises or forcing a lifetime commitment on you."

I dip my head quickly, waiting for the relief to set in, but it never comes. Was I really so naïve to think I'd find true love on *Hitched*?

Dax pats me on the shoulder and steers me toward the door. "Cheer up, sweetheart. I need you all smiles when the camera starts rolling."

"I'm totally fine—relieved even." I plaster a huge smile on my face and push my shoulders back. "When do we start?"

"The crew's almost all set up downstairs. When I give you the okay, come down and stand at the front door. The contestants will arrive one by one, and they'll make their introductions. Once everyone is here, the party will really get started."

"Party?" My voice rises a notch.

"Yes, it's a welcome ball. It'll be held in the west wing, ballroom number three."

There are multiple ballrooms on this property? Geez, I definitely need to do some exploring first thing in the morning. Assuming I survive the big fiesta.

Dax must notice my petrified expression because he gives me a reassuring smile. "Someone will escort you there. Don't worry, we won't let you get lost on the first day."

Tycen looks up from his phone as if suddenly remembering I'm there. "Okay, Kimmie-Jayne, we'll see you on the other side." He yanks the door open, and he and Dax disappear down the long corridor.

As soon as the door closes behind them, I resume my pacing. Five minutes to go. *You can do this, Kimmie-Jayne.* My stomach roils, and I'm scared I'm going to be sick. *No. No. No.* Trixie and Bash will kill me if anything happens to this dress. I hurry to the balcony and shove the sliding glass door open. Fresh air—I just need to breathe.

Outside, the sun dips into the ocean, vibrant yellows and oranges painting the evening sky. I suck in a breath, determined to focus on the beautiful landscape instead of my churning belly. At a distance, a flock of ginormous birds speckle the horizon. I peer into the darkening sky, wondering what kind of bird grows that large. There are at least two dozen of them, and they seem to be heading straight for the manor.

"Kimmie, it's go time." A voice inside pulls me away from the veranda. Stepping back into my room, a redhead pokes her head through the doorway. "You ready?"

I nod and rush over, lifting the tail of my gown so I don't trip. As the woman escorts me down the hallway, I try to figure out why she looks familiar. "Were you on the bus over from the studio?"

"Yes. And the plane."

"Oh, I'm sorry. I don't think we were ever introduced."

"That's okay. It's better that way; we're not supposed to mingle." She lowers her head and clutches her clipboard tighter.

That's what Cross said too. I'm not sure I like that. How can I pretend the crew doesn't exist?

I search her black blouse for a nametag but come up empty. "What's your name at least?"

"Sam. I'm the production assistant so you'll be seeing a lot of me. I basically do whatever Dax tells me."

"Gotcha. Well, nice meeting you, Sam."

She gives me a tight-lipped smile then stops when we reach the staircase. "As soon as you turn the corner down the steps, you'll be on camera. Make your way to the door and then wait. Don't forget to smile—always smile."

I inhale a quick breath. "Okay."

"Whenever you're ready." She motions to the first step, but I'm frozen in my tracks.

I wring my hands together, digging my nails into my skin. I feel like I'm standing on the edge of a precipice about to tumble into a pit full of snakes. Only they're not snakes, they're twenty-five eligible bachelors that I should be excited to meet.

A hand nudges my back, and I take a step forward, then another. As soon as I turn the corner, warm hazel eyes appear beside the blinking light of the camera.

Cross shoots me an indulgent smile, and my feet begin to move. Everything else falls away, and I focus only on the kind sparkle of his eyes.

Finally, reaching the door, I exhale a breath I hadn't realized I'd been holding and lean against the thick oak. From the corner of my eye, I allow myself a quick peek at the crew. On the opposite side of Cross is another camera operator, plus a few other guys dressed in black operating the lights and sound equipment. With the glare of the floodlight, I can barely make out more than shadowy forms.

"Action!" I recognize Dax's voice from a distance, and I turn my focus away from the crew and out to the lawn, plastering a huge smile on my face.

CHAPTER 8

The clip-clop of hooves echo down the long driveway, and I peer over the darkening landscape, squinting. The rolling terrain levels out and a white stallion appears, trotting along gracefully. I take a step further, straining to focus on the man seated atop the elegant steed, but my gaze falters on the feathery wings jutting out of the horse's midsection.

What in the world?

The wings spread open, revealing a rainbow of colors underneath. Vibrant reds, purples, blues and yellows burst from the feathery appendages.

My head whips from side to side trying to find Cross. He's no longer inside but has moved to film the approaching bachelor and faces away from me. I attempt to focus on the man once again, but this time I'm distracted by the golden horn protruding from the snowy creature's head.

Is this guy riding a freakin' unicorn with wings?

The majestic animal reaches the circular driveway and slows its pace, as if relishing the attention of the camera. I must be getting Punk'd—there's no other explanation. It all makes sense now; why *I* was chosen. They're messing with me.

An insane bout of the giggles bubbles up in my chest, and before I can help it I buckle over laughing.

"Cut!" Dax's sharp cry makes my spine rigid, and I straighten. He stalks over, his purple eyes blazing—no, I think they're actually glowing. "What in all the realms are you doing, sweetheart?"

I sweep the hysterical tears away and punch him in the arm. "This was funny, Dax. You got me, all right. Where's Ashton Kutcher? Is this a remake of *Punk'd* or what?"

I suddenly realize everyone's gone silent. Even the unicorn or whatever the heck he is, isn't moving. I search for Cross, but he's hiding behind the camera's tripod.

Dax smirks and throws his hands in the air. "I assure you, this is not *Punk'd*. It's just as described: one girl and twenty-five bachelors searching for love."

My eyes widen, and I point at the white animal. "Then what the heck is that?"

His jaw clenches almost imperceptibly before it relaxes. "It's theatrics, sweetheart. We stuck a fancy horn on a white horse and gave him animatronic wings. The theme for the welcome ball is Fantasy Island. I wanted it to be a surprise, but now you'll just have to fake it."

My cheeks burn as embarrassment steamrolls over me. I'm surely ten shades redder than my dress now. Of course this is all for show. There's nothing real about this reality TV program.

"I'm sorry," I say, covering my face with my hands.

"It's not your fault, sweetheart. Someone—I should've told you." He adjusts the sunglasses atop his head and shoots a narrowed glare at Sheppard, who I now recognize in the distance.

I want to smack myself for being so stupid. Any seasoned Hollywood actress would've simply played along. I vow to keep my questions to myself from now on, no matter how ridiculous the situation seems.

Dax backs away, out of the camera shot and motions to the crew. "Take two."

The clip-clop of the horse's hooves draws my attention once again, and my gaze falls on the most gorgeous male I've ever laid eyes on. Now that I've seen *him,* the unicorn pales in comparison.

He passes the marble fountain, stops at the foot of the steps and slides off the steed with the agility of an acrobat. Fiery golden eyes peer up at me from beneath a shock of dark chestnut hair. A hint of a smile plays along his full lips as he strides toward me with a deep purple rose in hand, his wide shoulders narrowing down to a tapered waist.

I swallow thickly as his large hand takes mine. Heat flows from his skin, wrapping my fingers in a warm fire. "Fenix Skyraider, at your service." His deep voice rumbles in his chest, doing funny things to my insides. He offers me the exotic flower and dips his head into a bow. I'm half-tempted to curtsy, but think better of it since it's highly likely I'll end up on my butt.

"Nice to meet you," I squeak. "Um… thanks for being here and for the flower."

He chuckles and proceeds inside.

Once he's out of sight, I realize a line of horses—er, unicorns, is making its way up the drive as dusk settles over the manor. I still can't get over how real they look. Narrowing my eyes, I try to focus on the point where the super-realistic wings attach to the horse but the saddle covers it.

The second guy descends from his mount, and I'm certain I've lost my mind now. I glance over my shoulder into the foyer and confirm Fenix is still inside. How could he be in two places at once?

"The name's *Flare* Skyraider. I believe you had the displeasure of meeting my older and less attractive twin." He winks, and my eyes settle on his deep green eyes. Flecks of emerald swirl through his irises, dancing under the flickering lantern overhead. He takes my hand and deposits a quick kiss. Heat unfurls from the top of my hand and travels over every inch of me. *Holy shnike's*!

"Nice to meet you." I hazard another glance at him and pray my cheeks aren't flaming. Besides the difference in eye color, he and Fenix are identical, from their pouty lips to arched brows, they're towering twin gods of hotness.

That's not going to make things difficult…

Another dozen guys introduce themselves, each arriving on a "unicorn" and one hotter than the next. Where did they find all these gorgeous men, and why didn't any of them exist back in Missouri?

There's Logan, Nix, Fraser, Elrian, Colt, Easton… And on and on. Their names and beautiful faces tangle in my mind.

I'm not sure my heart can take much more of this. I lean against the door for support as another handsome bachelor approaches. What catches my attention is the bucking steed underneath him. While each unicorn so far has trotted gracefully up the driveway, this one looks like he's got ants in his pants.

Yanking his mount to a halt, the jet-black-haired hunk mutters curses at the animal as he jumps off. From the looks of the fuming horse, he was about a second from being thrown off. The guy turns to me and catching my gaze, sighs and thrusts a hand through his unruly hair. Dark strands fall loose around his face, having come undone from the tie at the base of his neck. He glides toward me, all the awkwardness on the unicorn disappearing. His movements embody those of a panther. He flashes me a wicked smile as he adjusts his black tie, which blends into his all black suit. The only bit of color, a splash of deep red from the kerchief nestled in his suit pocket. He ascends the final step.

Suddenly, he's everywhere, his spicy cinnamon and clove scent crashing over me. Chilly fingers entwine with mine and soft lips brush one cheek and then the other before a silky accented voice whispers, "My apologies, señorita, that blasted animal refused to cooperate with me." He steps back, and I can finally breathe again. "It is my distinct pleasure to lay eyes on a creature as beautiful as yourself. Lucíano Montenegro de la Piedra, at your command."

Lucíano, what?

His jet-black eyes sparkle, but his lips don't give away his obvious amusement at my speechlessness. "You may simply call me Lucíano, if that's easier."

"Okay, Lucíano." His name rolls off my tongue, and I hope I haven't butchered it. He pronounces the c like a "th" and there's no way my gringa tongue can pull that off. Working with Lupita and Hector, I've gotten pretty used to the Hispanic accent, but his is nothing like their Mexican one. It sounds old world, richer and more refined.

"I greatly anticipate the pleasure of speaking further inside." He drops a kiss on my hand and spins toward the entrance.

I can't help but watch his lithe form disappear under the archway. His feline moves have me completely mesmerized.

The clopping of unicorn hooves turns my attention back to the driveway and my next suitor.

The following bachelor has blonde hair almost as long as mine but neatly swept up in a tie at the base of his neck. Light stubble covers his chin and cheeks, giving him that sexy scruffy look. He extends his hand as he approaches and a slight breeze picks up, sending goose bumps over my skin. "Aren Carter, and it's a pleasure to finally meet you, Kimmie-Jayne." His voice is smooth like whiskey and just as sinful, but there's something sweet behind those twinkling navy irises.

"Nice to meet you, too." How are these guys so hot?

"Save me a dance tonight, okay?" He winks and releases my hand.

"Of course."

Aren crosses the threshold into the foyer, and I glance at the crowd of men already assembled. I'm either the luckiest or the unluckiest girl in America. What am I going to do with all of these guys?

Turning back to the driveway, I return my focus to the approaching unicorn. Bring on the next hottie.

Elijah, Klaus, Gunnar, Cillian, Ryder… I'm never going to remember all these names. Stunning men parade in front of me, and I feel like I've been dropped into a Mr. Universe Pageant.

Just when I don't think I can stuff one more name into my head, Dax yells, "Cut!"

For a second, his voice shocks me. I'd completely forgotten about them—the director, the camera, the crew. I'd been completely wrapped up in the guys. I spin around searching for Cross but only catch a glimpse of his retreating figure.

Sam rushes over and pats me on the shoulder. "Good job. Dax seemed happy with the opening scene."

"Thank goodness," I mutter on an exhale.

The rest of the crew moves inside, the clatter of camera, lighting equipment and muted chatter filling the air, while my head swarms with the names and faces of the twenty-five men I met.

"You okay?" asks Sam, motioning for me to follow her.

I must have made my confused face. "Yeah, I just don't

know how I'm going to keep all those guys straight." I finger the elegant lace along my sleeve, the soft material comforting.

She pulls the clipboard from her tote and hands me a stack of paper-clipped pages. "Headshots and bios. This should help."

I flip through the glossy sheets and smile. "Thank you so much. This is perfect." Beside each picture is a name and a short biography. This little cheat sheet is going to save my life.

Trixie and Bash appear in the foyer, and I'm giddy at the sight of them. I'd only spent a few hours with my stylists, but somehow I know we'll be fast friends.

"You were phenomenal!" Bash pulls me into a hug, his hands clapping my back excitedly.

Trixie yanks him off with a narrowed glare. "Don't mess up her makeup and get your guy smell all over her dress." For such a tiny girl, she has fierce written all over her.

Sam turns to my stylists, tucking her clipboard back in her bag and gives them what I'm discovering is her no-nonsense look. "You've got fifteen minutes for touch-ups, then Kimmie needs to be in ballroom three."

"Gotcha." Trixie tugs on my arm and I'm sandwiched between her and Bash, racing up the stairs before I have a second to catch my breath.

CHAPTER 9

Pounding bass reverberates down the long hall, shaking the gilded candelabras along the walls. The flames flicker with each beat, matching the fevered staccato of my pulse. A trickle of sweat snakes down my spine as I near the ballroom, and I hope it doesn't leave a wet mark down my gown. That would be embarrassing…

The gold in-laid doors swing open, and Cross steps into the corridor. He's dressed in all black with a headset and mic resting around his neck. Relief rushes over me at the sight of him. With all the craziness I've encountered in the last day, he brings a sense of normalcy—which is weird since I just met him. His presence is oddly comforting, and I resist the urge to wrap him in a big bear hug.

"You ready?" His gaze rakes over me, and he seems pleased. For some reason that makes me happy even though I keep telling myself it shouldn't.

"I wish you could go in there with me. I mean on the other side of the camera."

A wry grin splits his lips. "Nah. I wouldn't stand a chance

against those guys in there."

Sure, Cristian Cross isn't supermodel hot like the twenty-five guys I met, but he is definitely cute. He's the type of cute I'd grown up with in Missouri—boy next door, football player, sweet.

I bump my shoulder against his and give him a warm smile. "I wouldn't bet on that." If I hadn't been thrown into this show, Cross would've been exactly the kind of guy I could see myself dating. He is like a genuine needle in the haystack of posers in L.A.

He grunts and turns toward the door. "Before I open these and you freak out like with the unicorns, I want to warn you that what you're about to see is going to be a few notches up from the flying horses."

"Seriously?"

He nods. "They've really gone all out with this, um, fantasy theme."

"Okay, well thanks for the warning." I run my hands over the front of my dress to make sure all my parts are still hidden. I give Cross the okay and he stands to the side, pulling the doors open.

A whoosh of cool air wafts over me as a rainbow of lights explodes across the ballroom. The music intensifies as I step inside, the electrifying beats swirling through my veins. I'm not much of a dancer, and yet I can't help my body moving to the pounding rhythm. My eyes finally adjust to the prancing lights, and the unbelievable scene takes shape.

Outrageously costumed men and woman dance atop pedestals that jut high into the air. Tilting my head back, a man with the head of a tiger peers down at me, his green feline eyes aglow. Across the room an enormous aquarium makes up the back wall. Bright lights focus on the stunning mermaids swimming in the giant blue pool.

Unreal. I can't get my eyes to settle in one place.

A man flies over my head, his translucent wings reflecting the purple lights from above as three women zip across the room behind him. They move as if performing a mid-air dance, twirling and circling like prima ballerinas. Following their graceful movements higher, I can just make out a tightrope strung across the ballroom and various dangling swings. Not that I've ever seen Cirque du Soleil, but I imagine this is what their shows look like. Although I'm not sure that any of their performers *actually* fly.

A spotlight shines on my dress, quickly crawling up to my face. I only have a second to squint before the glaring light nearly blinds me. Another spotlight appears across the room, and a man in a white tux and top hat croons into a handheld microphone.

"Ladies and gentlemen, welcome! I am Methyss, your master of ceremonies for the evening." He turns to me with a raised hand. "Your princess has arrived, Miss Kimmie-Jayne Starr."

Applause fills the room, drowning out the deejay's electric beats, and I actually wish they'd turn up the music. Being the center of attention is not my forte. *Weird for an actress—I know.*

A striking man appears beside me and offers his arm. "May I have the honor of the first dance?"

I nod and thread my arm through his. As he walks me to the dance floor, my mind shuffles through the images of all the guys I met earlier. The golden blonde hair and sky blue eyes are definitely familiar, but for the life of me I can't remember his name.

The music slows and a well-muscled arm encircles my waist, drawing me into his chest. I rest my hands around his neck. It's a good thing Trixie forced me to wear the four-inch heels, or I'd never have reached. I sneak a peek up at him through my faux long lashes, hoping his name pops into my brain. How in the world did Cullen find so many hot guys for this show?

The man standing before me looks like he just fell from heaven. A strong Roman nose and perfectly sculpted cheekbones round out his angelic face. The fitted navy-blue suit highlights his wide shoulders and brings out the azure in his eyes.

His lip curls up as he catches me staring. "Are you enjoying your evening, Kimmie-Jayne?"

"Oh, yes. This is incredible." A multitude of names tumble around in my mind, but none of them are his. Chewing on my lower lip, I curse Dax for not making the guys wear nametags.

Blondie lifts a brow as his eyes rake over me. "I'll forgive you this one time, but I will admit, it isn't often a girl forgets my name."

"No, I, um..." *How the heck did he know*? I take a step back to regain my composure. The warmth of his arms around my waist makes it hard to form sentences.

"It's okay. I'm Cillian."

Silly Cillian—that's how I'll remember it.

He pulls me back into his arms and whispers, "Don't ever forget it." His warm breath ignites goose bumps up and down my arms, and I'm tempted to snuggle closer. Geez, I have to get a grip. I can't be falling all over myself in front of *every* one of these guys.

"So, Cillian, what made you want to enter this competition?" I'm proud of myself for getting a full sentence out.

He quirks a sexy brow. "Competition?" He grunts. "Please." His blue eyes sparkle, and it's like the stars appear across a sunlit sky.

For a second, I wonder if he's following a script with that cheesy line. "Well, you seem very sure of yourself."

He takes my hand and twirls me in a quick circle before he answers. My head spins before my hands land on his chest to steady myself. His very firm chest.

He dips his head so we're eye level and whispers, "It's not arrogance if it's the truth, angel." He shoots me a playful smile before spinning me out once again.

Laughing, I barrel right into the arms of another bachelor. Pale lilac eyes graze over me before moving over my shoulder.

"Thanks, Cillian." The guy nods at my scowling former dance partner. "You saved me the effort of asking to cut in."

This guy I do remember. His white-blonde hair and unusual eyes imprinted in my memory like a tattoo. Elrian.

"May I?" He dips into a bow, offering his hand.

I'm already practically in his arms, but the gesture is nice. "I'd love to."

Unlike the heat Cillian exudes, Elrian's skin is icy cool against mine. It actually feels nice—refreshing after the intense few hours. He surprises me as he breaks into a formal waltz. Luckily, my mama had insisted on cotillion so I'm able to match each of his intricate steps.

Elrian smiles down at me, his pale skin practically aglow under the rainbow of lights. "You surprise me, Miss Starr," he breathes as he whisks me across the dance floor.

I only now realize the crowd has made a circle around us, and the cameras are perched right outside of it.

"You surprise me, too. I didn't picture you as a waltzer."

He chuckles, revealing perfect white teeth. "Not all men are savages like the ones you find in L.A."

"Thank goodness for that."

He tips his head to the side. "Is that why you entered this competition—to find someone more suitable?"

"Yes, definitely. I know I'm a new actress in Hollywood, but I didn't do it only to be on TV." I shrug, realizing how naïve I must sound. Everyone knows struggling actors do reality TV to get a foot in the door. I find it hard to believe that these handsome men are in the same position.

"I think that's lovely and refreshing." He spins me around, and then lowers me into a dip.

For a moment, I forget there are dozens of people surrounding us and focus only on his calming lavender eyes. "Why did you come?" *Surely, he doesn't have a problem finding a date.*

His eyes grow serious, and he pulls me up so I'm standing in front of him once again. "My family believes it is time for me to marry, and so here I am."

Why does he sound upset about that?

Before I can ask, a big hand settles on my shoulder, whirling me around. "Can I cut in, lass?"

The deep baritone voice and thick accent has my stomach doing cartwheels before my eyes even have a chance to settle on the tall Scotsman before me.

Elrian frowns when I turn back to excuse myself, and I feel horrible, but this is the game, right?

"We'll talk later!" I shout over my shoulder as hottie McScottie drags me toward the bar.

"My, ye are a bonnie one, aren't ye?"

"Why, thank you."

His green eyes glimmer as they regard me. "Enough of the dancin', lass. It's time to get some booze in ye."

I can't argue with the man there. I stare at the towering highlander in full traditional Scottish plaid and wonder if the rumors are true. My eyes roam down to his hunter green kilt and heat flushes my cheeks.

He laughs, a big deep chuckle. "The rumors are true, lass. There's nothing under there besides what the good Lord blessed me with."

Now I'm the one laughing, and it isn't even in an uncomfortable way. There is something about Fraser that instantly puts me at ease. I felt it the first time I met him when he leapt off his unicorn.

"So what'll ye have?"

I want to say vodka and lots of it. Somehow I'm certain that's the only way I'll ever survive this show, but a little voice inside my head warns me that may not be the best idea ever.

"Rosé, please."

He flags down a bartender, and I will myself not to stare as the girl approaches. Light pink translucent wings flutter behind her as she floats toward us. *Man, what is the costume budget on this show?*

"What can I get you?" She sweeps short black hair behind her ear, revealing a very pointy tip.

"The lady will have a rosé, and I'll have yer best scotch." Fraser doesn't seem to find her pointed ears or fairy wings even a bit odd. Why am I the only one freaking out about this stuff? Their agents must have done a better job at filling them in on what to expect than Gianfranco had. With how fast everything happened, I suppose there wasn't any time. I'll simply play along like everyone else to avoid another unicorn fiasco.

In seconds, she's back with a drink in each hand. Before I can reach for mine, a large hand intercepts.

"Please, let me." A pair of intense onyx eyes fixes on mine, and my knees wobble. *Ack*, what's his name?

"Aw, come on, Ryder, I just got a moment with the wee lass," grumbles Fraser.

Right, Ryder!

He tips his watch at Fraser and clucks his teeth. "Sorry, time's up."

CHAPTER 10

Ryder Strong. What a name. It's like his parents knew he'd come out this way when they had him. Six and a half feet of muscled male stands before me, tattoos snaking up and down his massive arms. Unlike the other twenty-four bachelors, he'd driven up the manor in a sporty black motorcycle. Every inch of him screams bad boy, and every inch of me wants a taste. If only I can get my mouth to start working. His bottomless black irises drill into mine as I struggle to spit a word out.

"Cat got your tongue, little minx?"

I gulp down the rosé, wetting my dry throat. "It's just been a lot."

His lip twitches but doesn't break into a full smile. "I'm sorry you had to put up with all those guys pawing at you. I'm sure it's exhausting."

I giggle and lean up against the bar. "No, it's not that. I'm really happy to meet all of you. Everything is just happening so fast." I motion at the trapeze artists above. "And then there's all that."

He tilts his head up, arching a dark brow. "Pesky little flying creatures," he mutters. A flash of yellow streaks across his irises and for a second, I'm not sure if it's from the lights or actually from his eyes.

My mouth drops. "Huh?"

He shakes his head, tipping his bottle of beer back. "Nothing. You're right, it is a lot, but it is Hollywood after all."

I'm not sure how much more weirdness I can take. The police officers' conversation at Pollo Loco leaps to the forefront of my mind. I push it back, shaking my head. There's no such thing as supernatural creatures. I casually glance around the room, trying to catch Cross's eye but he's nowhere in sight. Am I allowed to yell cut?

"So..."

I turn back to Ryder, mentally chastising myself for being rude. "Sorry."

"You seem stressed. Maybe I can help you with that." He leans in and licks his lips, drawing closer.

My pulse picks up as his penetrating eyes narrow in on mine. A spark of yellow ignites in his pupils again, and my thoughts get hazy. The music slows, and everything around me blurs.

Ryder's arms encircle me. He pulls me closer, his eyes searing into me until my breaths become shallow. His lips are only inches away, and all I can think about is wanting them pressed against mine. Before they make contact, Ryder sucks in a deep breath and a light blue vapor escapes between my lips. He opens his mouth inhaling the strange haze.

A pang pricks my chest, and my lungs tighten. A part of me realizes this should hurt, but somehow I can't sense the pain. I don't feel anything anymore. It's like I'm completely weightless, floating away across a murky sky.

A dark hulking shadow appears over Ryder's shoulder, and

my newest suitor is wrenched away before I can blink. The fog in my mind begins to lift, and I recognize the twins standing between us. Each has a hand around one of Ryder's tattooed biceps. His eyes are wild as he tries to fight them off.

"Cut!"

My head spins, and I have the terrifying thought that I'm going to pass out—in front of everyone. My knees tremble, but before I fall, a familiar body is beside me.

Warm arms come around me, and I happily lean in. "Cross," I whisper. I cling to his chest as he shouts. His entire body is tense, his muscles strained and I can't understand why.

Someone hands me a shot glass filled with dark crimson liquid. "Drink it, *amor*." The thick Spanish accent is familiar so I accept the offering, chugging the nasty metallic-tasting fluid.

The fogginess immediately clears, and the shadowy figure before me coalesces to form Lucíano. Cross passes me into the hot Latino's arms, and the cameraman's angry yells amplify.

Cross pummels into Ryder, grabbing him by the collar. Fenix and Flare release him and back away as curses fly from Cross's mouth. "I should have your ass for this. You know that crap is forbidden." He curls his fingers into a fist and pulls his arm back.

Dax's spikey purple hair appears across my vision, and it's like he's everywhere all at once. I rub my eyes, forcing them to focus. He yanks Cross off Ryder before he releases the punch and separates the two men with his wide wingspan. Pointing at Ryder, Dax snarls, "One warning. That's all you get. Next time you pull a stunt like that, you're out. I don't care who your father is."

Ryder sneers and adjusts his crumpled shirt, then raises his hands. "It was an accident. I didn't mean to hurt the girl; I swear it. It's like I lost control..." He sniffs his beer, raising a brow, and then tosses it to the ground. The bottle shatters, sending glass flying across the dance floor. His eyes meet mine, and he mouths, "I'm sorry." I turn away, burying my face in Lucíano's chest. His spicy scent is like heaven to my addled mind.

What the blazes just happened?

Ryder storms off with a grunt, and Fenix and Flare follow close behind him. The twins shoot me a reassuring smile before they disappear into the crowd.

I only now realize that everything's gone silent. The music has stopped, the acrobats are standing around us in a circle and even the bartenders have stopped pouring drinks.

Cross rotates in my direction, but before he can reach me, Dax grabs his arm. He hauls him off the dance floor, and my heart plummets.

I try to squirm out of Lucíano's arms, but he holds me tight.

"Let go of me. I need to talk to Cross."

"I'm sorry, amor, but I'm afraid that's impossible." He twirls me around to face him and tilts my chin up. His dark eyes lock onto mine, and my mind swims once again. "Go back to your room and rest. You will remember everything about this evening except for that unfortunate encounter with Ryder. You had a wonderful time, and everyone adored you."

A smile splits my lips, and I have no idea why. Lucíano regards me for a moment before releasing me into another pair of arms. These are slender and petite, even more so than my own.

"Trixie?"

"Hey, girl. You ready to call it a night?"

I bob my head up and down. *I'm so ready*. A strange sensation niggles at my gut that I'm forgetting something, but I let the exhaustion win out. The idea of crawling into my ginormous canopied bed is too good to pass up.

A SEVERE POUNDING in my skull wakes me much too early, and I roll over to check the clock. Not even seven yet. *Stupid rosé.* The cameras don't start rolling until nine so I yawn and pull the covers up over my head.

I squeeze my eyes shut hoping to get another hour of sleep, but it's no use. Images from last night's fantasy ball flash through my mind like an old movie reel. How in the world did they pull that stuff off? The flying, the mermaids, the unicorns… I make a mental note to ask Cross next time I see him.

I wish I could talk to someone about everything, but I signed away my rights to disclose anything about the show in the contract. I can't even tell my parents where I am until *Hitched* airs. I suppose I'm lucky I'm allowed to talk to them at all. That reminds me I need to check in on my dad. I shoot Mom a quick text message, and I'm relieved to hear he's back home on bed rest. With the five-hour time difference, I hadn't had a chance to talk to them yet. *Hold on, Dad, just two more months, and you'll never have to work again.*

With a huff, I push the blankets back and trudge toward the bathroom. As I walk past the balcony, the ocean glitters with the first rays of sun. It's too beautiful not to admire so I slide the glass doors open and inhale a breath of salty air. Behind the clouds, large shadows fly across the sky.

It's those huge birds again. A massive flock of them soar in the distance, dipping and twirling across the brightening blue. Another thing to add to my list of questions for Cross—or Trixie and Bash for that matter. It won't be long before my stylists appear to make me up for the day.

Am I ready for another day? I can't help shake the feeling that something is off.

Happy thoughts of the night before flicker through my mind. All of the guys had been sweet and very welcoming. There really is no need for me to be nervous—except about the idea of having to choose one. How will I ever pick?

After only one night, I am more confused than ever. Sighing, I close the balcony doors and head to the bathroom. After a hot shower, I'll make some notes on the cheat sheet Sam gave me.

I step into the adjoining bathroom, and a scream tears from my lips.

Blood streams down the pristine marble countertop, pooling in a large puddle on the floor. I clap my hand over my mouth to keep from shrieking again as my gaze focuses on the severed head of a white unicorn—er, horse atop the counter.

Footsteps thunder down the corridor, and the front door of my room whips open, smacking against the wall. Two of the bachelors race in, their eyes wide as they settle on the scene. Klaus and Gunnar, I think.

My chest heaves and I force the nausea back down my throat, spinning away from the gruesome scene.

One of the guys curses and tugs me out of the bathroom. I'm frozen, unable to move for some reason. Strong arms wind themselves around me, but a chill snakes its way up my back nonetheless.

"It's going to be okay, darling." I glance up at my protector, and warm amber eyes look down on me. Yes, Klaus. I didn't get to talk to him at the party, but I remember the scruffy beard and man bun from the introductions.

The other guy slams the bathroom door shut and stands before me. I must have seemed confused because he offers me an indulgent smile. "It's Gunnar."

I nod blankly.

More footfalls sound in the hallway and now half the crew

fills up my bedroom, making the huge room feel cramped. I'm suddenly very aware of my flimsy tank top and short pink shorts.

"What the hell happened?" Dax makes it to me first, followed by Sheppard and Tycen. Dax shouts into a Bluetooth speaker I hadn't even noticed dangling from his ear. "Make sure all cameras are off. Now."

I can't help but notice that Cross is missing.

Gunnar opens the bathroom door to show the others in, and I bury my face in Klaus's chest. I don't ever want to see that again. A wave of muttered gasps fills the air.

That poor horse. Who would do such a terrible thing?

"Son of a b—" Sheppard cuts off the curse when he sees my terrified face. He points at Tycen. "Get her out of here until this is cleaned up."

Tycen shuffles me out of the room with Klaus and Gunnar at my heels. He leads us to the sitting area that separates my wing from where the guys live. I slump down on the couch and tug at the bottom of my shorts, wishing they covered more leg.

Tycen sits across from me, meticulously dressed as always. How was he already in a suit at this hour?

Two warm bodies sit on either side of me, and the chill racing through me relents. Though I haven't spent much time with either of these guys, I'm comforted by their presence. Tycen is like a cold fish.

Klaus's hand squeezes my knee. "Are you all right?"

"Yeah, I think so."

"What exactly happened?" Tycen's tone is all business as usual.

"I have no idea. I woke up and found the poor animal like that." I bury my face in my hands, trying to push away the horrible image permanently seared into my brain.

Gunnar grunts. "Whoever did that was a professional. They

knew exactly what they were doing. Uni—horses aren't an easy kill."

Tycen shoots him a veiled glare.

Gunnar stutters and clears his throat. "I like to hunt in my spare time," he says to me.

Bleh. I mentally strike him off the list. How anyone could get off on hunting innocent animals is beyond me.

"What kind of show are you running here?" Klaus stiffens beside me, moving to the edge of his seat. "Ryder last night and now this?" A low growl echoes in his throat.

Ryder… for some reason his name rings a bell. I vaguely remember a pleasant conversation with a hot guy and more rosé.

"Keep it together, Klaus," Tycen hisses, his back straightening as he shifts to the edge of the cushion. "We'll have a team investigate and get to the bottom of this right away."

"I hope so," adds Gunnar, his pale blue eyes lighting up. "I didn't plan on making this a working trip. But it can be if necessary."

Tycen nods as if he knows exactly what he's referring to. Meanwhile, I'm hopelessly lost—as usual.

"Where's Cross?" I mumble. He's the only one that will give me the answers I need. Or at least I hope he will.

"He's working on something for Shep. Finnerty will be manning the main rig today."

"We're still filming after what happened?" My heart rate picks up a notch.

Tycen stands and re-buttons his jacket. "The show must go on, as they say."

Dax appears around the corner, his purple spiky hair shooting in odd angles as an objection sits poised on the tip of my tongue. What if one of the bachelors is responsible for that horse? Someone snuck into my room in the middle of the night—it could have been my head in there.

"Sweetheart, how are you holding up?" Dax slides in between Gunnar and me, slipping his arm around my shoulder. "How's my little star?"

"I'm a little shaken up, Dax. I'm not going to lie." I peer into his lilac irises, the unique color holding me spellbound as always. "Tycen told me we're still shooting today. Are you sure that's safe?"

"Of course it is, sweetheart. I'm very sorry you were frightened, but I'm afraid that was nothing more than a juvenile prank."

"A prank?" I shoot up. I'd almost had a heart attack.

He suppresses a smile, but it creeps along his lips anyway. "It wasn't a real horse. It was only one of the animatronic heads we use to create the unicorns." He shrugs. "You know how immature men can be."

"It wasn't real?" My voice squeaks.

"No, sweetheart. You were never in any real danger."

"Who did this? It was still completely out of line." Gunnar stands by my side, and I reconsider my hasty decision of scratching him off the list.

Dax lifts a hand, and Gunnar backs off with a snarl. "I assure you the person has been dealt with."

"How?" I square my shoulders at the director. "And how did you find out who did it so quickly?"

"It was bachelor number thirteen – Cort Greenley. He's being escorted off the island as we speak."

My mind flips through the images of all the men, but comes up blank for this guy. How could someone come up with such a cruel prank?

"And we found him because we have cameras all over the property, as I'm sure you understand."

"So why would he do something so stupid?" Klaus crosses his arms over his muscled chest. In my panicked state, I hadn't even noticed how ripped he is.

Dax shrugs. "I'll be sure to have a talk with Cullen. He is the casting director, after all. He must have missed something." He turns to me, his cat eyes smiling. "I promise everything will go swimmingly today. Tonight is a big night—the first elimination round."

My heart sinks like a rock. "So soon? It's only been a day."

"I'm afraid so." He squeezes my shoulder. "But look at the bright side, since we already sent Cort home, you only have to eliminate nine men tonight."

Nine? I didn't think I could even name that many.

CHAPTER 11

"Oh my goddess, you poor little thing." Bash tightens his arms around me as I blubber, recounting the horrific events of the morning.

Trixie rubs my back, squishing me in between the two of them. "I'm sorry we didn't come sooner, but no one told us until now."

"Where do you guys live anyway?" My screams had woken practically the whole manor. Bash releases me, and I slump down on the bed. I'm beyond happy to have them here with me, and I wish they could stay in my wing forever.

Bash dramatically rolls his eyes. "With staff, on the other side of the property."

"Maybe you guys can move into my room. I don't think I'll ever be able to sleep there again." We currently sit in the extra bedroom of my wing. It isn't quite as big or fancy as the master, but it's more than enough for me. At this point, I'd rather sleep on the floor than in that grisly room.

"I doubt Shep would allow that." Trixie sits beside me and strokes my hair. "They're pretty strict about us keeping our distance from *the talent*." She throws air quotes around the last word, and I can't help but laugh.

Bash glances at his watch and squeals. "We have to get a move on, ladies. Camera rolls in thirty minutes." He rushes over to the closet where he and Trixie had lugged over half of my new clothes. This one isn't big enough to hold everything from the other one.

"So what am I doing today?"

"Just more casual group interactions—" says Bash.

Trixie cuts him off. "Poolside!"

I cringe, frowning. Even though I knew the moment would come, I didn't think it would be so soon. The idea of parading around in a bikini in front of twenty-five—scratch that—twenty-four guys and tons of cameras is my idea of hell.

"Oh stop, you're gorgeous." Bash pinches my cheek before disappearing into the closet. Was I that easy to read or did everyone in this place have psychic abilities?

Thirty minutes later, I'm suited up and walking down the long corridor. The camera starts rolling as soon as I hit the staircase and nervous butterflies take flight in my belly. Bash insisted on platform sandals, and as I teeter on the edge of the steps, I'm mentally cursing him.

I move forward, praying I don't tumble down the staircase and flash my butt to the world when a long whistle breaks the silence. The twins appear around the corner, and I recognize a few of the other guys crowding around them. More whistles and catcalls fill the air and though heat rushes up my neck, the tension subsides and I crack a smile.

When I reach the landing, Flare offers me his arm, which I gladly accept. Secretly, I hope his hulking form will hide mine. As if reading my thoughts, Fenix takes my other arm and now I'm sandwiched between the towering twins.

Flare leans in, his warm breath tickling my ear. "I'm sorry you didn't get to dance with me last night."

I giggle as goose bumps tingle down my arm. "Me too." Why didn't I dance with him? For some reason, I don't remember much at all about the night.

"You didn't miss much," snorts Fenix. "My brother is a terrible dancer. He would've stomped all over your toes."

"Don't listen to him, firecracker." Flare pulls me into his side, and the smoky scent of a crackling fire consumes me. "He's just jealous."

We pass through glass French doors, and the incredible backyard unfurls before us. It's like I've stepped onto a five-star resort with the infinity pool and swirling jacuzzis. A full-size bar juts out of the center of the pool—the island music and thatched roof reminding me of a postcard from a tropical paradise.

A man tends the bar, and I immediately recognize his sweeping blue hair blowing in the breeze. Elijah. He tucks the wayward strands behind his ears and whirls a cocktail shaker between his hands. His bottom half is covered by the counter, but I can't take my eyes off his upper body. Wide shoulders taper down to a well-muscled chest, and a beautiful conch hangs from a cord around his neck.

The sound of Flare clearing his throat tears me away from my blatant ogling. "Damn sirens," he mutters.

"He's a mer—" Fenix cuts himself off when I turn to face him.

"What was that?"

He shakes his head. "Nothing." He shoots me a wicked grin. "My brother can't handle a little friendly competition."

The twins escort me to a lounger and take a seat on either side of me. A second later, a young guy in a gray uniform appears with a tray of champagne flutes. Fenix passes one to me, and takes one for himself, completely ignoring his brother.

"Nice," grumbles Flare as he grabs one before the server moves on.

Almost in unison, Flare and Fenix tug their shirts over their heads, and I nearly choke on my sip of champagne. Besides their gloriously ripped torsos, each has an enormous dragon tattoo across their chest. Fenix's is impossibly golden and practically matches the unique gold hue of his eyes. While Flare's is an emerald green, also identical to his irises.

"Wow." I can't help myself, the word pops out of my mouth as my gaze rakes over their bodies.

Both guys grin shamelessly.

"Those are pretty amazing." I lean toward Flare to get a closer look.

"Yeah, I know. I work out."

I dig my elbow into his belly and hit hard packed steel. "I was talking about the tattoo."

He chuckles. "Oh. I guess that's cool too."

"So you guys got them together?"

Fenix drags his lounge chair closer, and the dragon dances across his chest. "Something like that."

A shadow blocks out the sun, and I gaze up into a pair of blue eyes, golden blonde hair rimming his head like a halo. "Kimmie-Jayne, so nice to see you again."

"You too, Cillian." I'm proud of myself for remembering his name this time. I'm pretty sure it would've killed him if I hadn't.

He folds his large body onto my lounge chair, his massive thighs rubbing against my leg.

"Aw, come on, Cillian. Wait your turn," Flare grumbles.

He turns his bright-eyed gaze at the younger twin. "I don't

think so. The two of you monopolized her the entire walk over. It's my turn."

Flare and Fenix rise muttering curses as they head toward the pool. The sun's warm rays caress my skin, and I'm sure I'll be following behind them before long.

Cillian pulls his shirt off and sits back against the lounge chair, tugging me between his legs.

Oh!

"Relax, angel," he whispers as he begins to massage my shoulders. "After the morning you've had, you deserve some pampering."

My shoulder blades slacken, and I lean into his firm chest as a groan slips out. His fingers are like magic, pressing and kneading the stress away. My eyes close without my consent, and I'm surprised by how at ease I am around Cillian. He didn't strike me as the considerate type when we first met last night. Cocky and arrogant—yes.

"In response to your question yesterday, I'm here for the same reason everyone else is—to woo you."

"Well, you're doing a great job so far," I breathe out. My entire body feels weightless, like he's removed every ounce of anxiety holding me down.

He chuckles, and my head bounces up and down on his chest. The sound sets off a surge of warmth in my belly.

"Oy! No fair, he can't touch the lass. Not all of us have his special powers."

I open my eyes, squinting against the sun to see a grinning Scotsman. An adorable dimple peeks through his five o'clock shadow, and I can't even be mad at him for ruining the tranquil moment.

He sits on the lounge beside us, clad in only his kilt and swirls the ice cubes in the glass clenched in his hand. "You all right after this morning, lass? It's terrible what happened."

I nod and sit up, slightly uncomfortable at being sprawled on top of one guy with another one so nearby. "Did either of you guys know Cort—the guy who did it?"

They both shake their heads in unison.

"I'm not here to make friends," Cillian growls.

"That's probably a good thing, laddie."

I suppress a laugh as Fraser winks at me.

"Laddie? Please I'm easily twice your age." Cillian stiffens behind me, and my sense of tranquility vanishes.

"Depends how ye're countin'." Fraser gulps down his drink and stretches his long legs out.

Cillian ticks his head toward Fraser's kilt as a frown curls his lips. "Careful you don't let anything slip out, highlander. None of us signed up for that."

Fraser lets out a big belly laugh and crosses his legs. "No, I reckon ye didn't. And I sure don't want to scare the bonnie lass."

Heat seeps into my cheeks as I imagine in way too much detail what's hidden underneath that kilt. The building heat travels through my veins, and I shoot up before I turn fifty shades of red. "I think I'm going to jump into the pool." *And cool off.*

I dive into the deep end, the cool water enveloping me in its chilly embrace. Immediately, my body temperature normalizes, and my racing hormones take a chill pill. I swim as long as I can underwater until my lungs begin to burn. Emerging at the opposite side of the pool, a pair of blue eyes catches mine from the tiki bar.

"I've been waiting for you to come say hi." Elijah pours bright blue liquid into a martini glass.

I swim over and perch up on the underwater bar stool. "How'd you get stuck behind the bar?"

He tosses his electric blue hair over his shoulder. "I volunteered."

"Is that what you do back in L.A.?"

"One of the many." He grins and downs the drink he just served. "Can I get you something?"

The bubbles from the champagne already have my head slightly spinning, but after the morning I had, I decide it's okay to indulge. "I'll have a mimosa." I just realize I skipped breakfast—at least a mimosa has orange juice to provide some nourishment.

"Coming right up, beautiful." He pops the champagne cork, making a show of it and squeezes fresh orange juice into the flute—with his bare hands. Somehow, he makes it look super sexy.

Handing it to me, his fingers graze mine and my skin tingles from his touch. How is it possible that all of these guys have such an effect on me? And how will I eliminate nine of them by tonight?

CHAPTER 12

The creepy black bird eyes me as he paces the length of the cage and lets out a shrill squawk. The hairs on the back of my neck rise, and I turn my gaze from the crow to Dax, snapping my jaw back into place. "I'm supposed to do *what* with this thing?"

When Dax and Sam showed up at my room to prep me for the elimination ceremony, this was *so* not what I'd expected.

"It's easy, sweetheart." Dax spears me with his smiling lavender gaze. "The bird knows exactly what to do. Simply whisper the bachelor's name into Obsidian's ear and whether he's staying or going."

"Where's his ear?" I squeal. Do birds even have ears?

Sam moves out from behind Dax's shadow and opens the cage door. She clucks at the unnerving creature, and he perches on her finger. Extending her arm, she holds him a few inches away from me. "Kimmie-Jayne meet Obsidian—or Obi as I like to call him."

Obi squawks again, eyeing me with his beady black eyes. "So he's like a trained bird or something?" I reach my hand out to touch him, and he snaps his beak. I jump back like a huge chicken and scrape my heel against the bedframe.

Sam nods, stifling a laugh as I grimace through the pain. "We've worked with him in the past. He's a little temperamental, but once the camera starts rolling, he's all business."

I arch a brow, still fairly certain the little bugger's going to bite my finger off.

Sam inches the bird closer to me. "Go on, give it a try."

Leaning in toward the creature, I whisper, "Dax: no."

The crow unfurls its wings and flies over to the bed, picking up a pin in its dark beak. Then he glides across the room and lands on Dax's shoulder, dropping the black pin in his hand.

I shake my head, my mouth hanging open again. Unbelievable.

"You understand how the pins work, right?" Dax pops back into the conversation, and the crow returns to its cage.

I glance down at the tray of thirty metal pins propped on my bed and run my finger over the cool metal. Three rows of ten pins each—each line unique. The first row of pins is gold with an interlocking infinity symbol, the second is silver with the image of a red-horned cupid, and the last line is black, an ominous skull and crossbones.

The last row is pretty self-explanatory—skull means you're out. That one I got. I still don't quite understand the infinity symbol or the chubby cupid.

"Sam, go over them one more time." Dax ticks his head at the tray and walks away with his phone to his ear.

She lifts the tray off the bed and holds it out to me. "If you really like the guy, give him the gold one."

I pick up the gold pin and examine it more closely. "What's the mark mean?"

"It's the soul mate symbol." She glances up at me and must

read the curiosity in my eyes. "It's from some ancient tribe of Druids or something." She waves her hand in the air and signals at the next row. "Silver—or the devilish cupids for maybe. You like him well enough, but you're not ready to pick out matching china yet. And the skull and crossbones for the guys you want out."

"Out but not dead, right?" I'm only halfway joking. With the way things have been going lately, I can't help but confirm.

She smirks and sets the pins back down on the bed. "Definitely not dead."

For some reason, I want to ask more about the soul mate stuff, but Dax rushes over and tugs on Sam's arm. "All set?"

I plaster on a fake smile. "Yup." Meanwhile, anxiety churns my stomach. I still have no idea who I'm eliminating. I'm such a procrastinator.

"Okay, we'll see you downstairs in thirty minutes. Someone will be up to escort you."

I nod at Dax, secretly hoping its Cross. I haven't seen him since last night and a weird hollowness has taken root in my chest.

Dax and Sam rush out, and the slam of the door behind them leaves me empty. It's ironic to feel alone in a house surrounded by twenty-four guys plus a full staff. Maybe I need to start spending more time in the other wing. Am I even allowed to do that?

Everything has been such a rush so far, and I still have so many unanswered questions.

I catch my reflection in the mirror as I walk to the desk where I stashed the bachelor cheat sheet. Tucking it under my arm, I gaze at the woman standing before me. Becky Sue would never believe it if she saw me—her little sister in a designer ball gown worth more than her husband's new/used Chevy. The silky emerald fabric clings to my body until it reaches my knees, then it flares out reminiscent of a mermaid's tail.

A few wisps of blonde hair dangle free from the elaborate up-do Bash and Trixie concocted, and I sweep them behind my ears. Smoky eye shadow and dark liner bring out my bright blue eyes, and I make a mental note to thank Trixie next time I see her. She's an absolute magician with makeup. I've never been very good at that stuff.

A rush of activity downstairs draws my attention away from the mirror, and I glance up at the clock. *Blast it*! Only twenty more minutes, and I still have no idea who to eliminate.

I plop down on the bed and flip through the pages of glossy pictures and bios. Next to the handsome faces are handwritten notes I added along the way. It was the only way to keep them straight in my head. Though I'd met all of the guys one way or another, there were definitely some that I'd spent more time with. These are the guys that stick out in my mind, and the ones I'll most likely keep.

After a lengthy deliberation, I quickly mark exes by the ones I hadn't had much of a chance to talk to. It isn't really fair, but it is all I can do. I make a short list of the keepers on the back of the last page—in no particular order.

1. Fenix
2. Flare
3. Klaus
4. Ryder
5. Elrian
6. Fraser
7. Lucíano
8. Cillian
9. Elijah

10. Gunnar
11. Aren
12. Logan
13. Nix
14. Colt
15. Easton

AT THE LAST MINUTE, I add a few of the guys I haven't gotten much of a chance to talk to as "maybes". They'll get the cute devil cupid pin. Colt's bio says he's a veterinarian, and I love animals so I decide to keep him. Easton barely spoke to me after the introductions, but there's something about his smile that makes me want to know more. Logan and Nix are simply gorgeous—I wish I had a better reason, but I have to at least be honest with myself.

That means the remaining nine bachelors get the skull and crossbones. I glance at the creepy black and white pins, and a pang of guilt swirls in my belly. *It's just a game.* I press the stack of pages against my chest and take a big breath.

Done.

CHAPTER 13

The sweeping atrium is silent as I enter, the click clack of my heels echoing across the space. The intense beating of my heart roars across my eardrums as I take in the decadent space. Tall glittering candelabras ring the room, roses of every color adorn each corner, seemingly flowing from the walls themselves. I walk the remaining few feet to the raised table holding my breath. Atop the deep red tablecloth sits the tray of pins and beside it, Obsidian in his gilded cage.

He caws, cocking his head to the side as I approach. His beady little eyes bore into me, but it's easier to look at him than the twenty-four men on the platform across the way. Cross never showed; one of the other assistants came to fetch me, and I can't help but wonder where he is.

A man with a sleek top hat approaches me, drawing my thoughts back to my current predicament. It takes me a second to recognize him as the master of ceremonies from the party last night. He gives me a crooked smile and escorts me to the middle of the hall. His skin is so tan there's an orange glow about it, perfectly matching the Gatorade-orange hair spilling out from underneath his tall hat.

"You ready?" he mutters under his breath.

I force my gaze away from his flamboyant hair. "Umhmm."

Releasing me, he turns toward the bachelors, and I'm finally compelled to look at them. The sea of beautiful faces blurs as dread compresses my lungs. I suck in a sharp breath, coercing my failing organs to keep pumping air.

Bright lights snap on, flooding the room in a neon glow and Dax's voice rings out from the shadows, "Action!"

Methyss raises his hands, and all eyes turn toward him. "Welcome, gentlemen. In case you've forgotten, the name's Methyss, and I have the pleasure of emceeing this momentous occasion. The first of many for some, the one and only for nine of you poor souls."

A hushed murmur rolls over the crowd.

I keep my focus on the floor, but every so often my eyes betray me, landing on one of the men across the way. Guilt seeps into me as I meet the gazes of those I've already mentally eliminated.

Flare and Fenix stand next to each other, each with shoulders pulled back. Flare winks at me, and my heart rate picks up a notch. *Yup. I definitely made the right decision keeping him.* The corner of Fenix's lip curls up and warmth fills my chest. *Both of them.*

"And now for the rules." Methyss' voice snaps me away from the twins' sexy smiles. "Ms. Kimmie-Jayne will reveal her decision to Obsidian." He pauses and points at the bird. "The crow will fly to each one of you and gift you a pin. If you receive the gold infinity pin, approach the platform to greet Ms. Starr then move to your right. If you get the silver cupid pin, you may greet her and then step to the left. Finally, if you find yourself the unlucky recipient of the black skull and crossbones, you may leave through the front door. A vehicle will be waiting to escort you off the property."

All eyes move toward the elaborate double doors, and I swallow hard. *I won't even get a chance to say goodbye to the ones I eliminate.* A part of me feels bad, but the other half is relieved I won't have to face them.

"As a reminder, gentlemen, we expect you'll all be on your best behavior—even if you are eliminated. There will be no uncalled for outbursts, fighting, or other shenanigans. Keep the pouting and crying to yourselves. And now, we will begin." Methyss tips his hat to me, revealing a bright orange tuft of hair. The ridiculous color incites a nervous giggle, but I quickly quash it down. At least it eases the growing tension as I take a step toward the cage.

The door creaks open and Obsidian flies out, landing on my arm. His large claws wrap around my bare shoulder, digging into my skin. I suppress the urge to squeal and instead clasp my hands together to steady the trembling.

Obi struts back and forth on my arm, his head bobbing as I struggle to get the words unstuck at the back of my throat.

Methyss shoots me a glance, raising his light eyebrows.

"Okay, okay," I mouth. Raising Obi to my eye level, I whisper into where I think his ear is. A second later, his large wings flap, the air ruffling the wisps of hair around my face. I sputter to get a strand unstuck from my lip-gloss and by the time I look up, the crow has landed on Elrian's shoulder.

Elrian tenses, his pale skin shimmering like porcelain under the bright lights. The bird drops the pin into his palm, and a small smile creeps along my suitor's face. The heavy silence dissipates as he makes his way through the guys.

He nods when he reaches me, placing the pin in the lapel of his fine powder-blue suit. "Thank you," he breathes.

I move forward to give him a hug or something, but

awkwardness holds me back. Elrian looks so formal, his white-blonde hair flawlessly gelled back, and I'm afraid to mess up the perfection. Maybe that's what made me choose him—I want to find out what's underneath that cold shell.

He dips his head and moves to the right.

Obi has returned to the table, and he's pacing back and forth. His dark eyes find mine, and I swear he's rushing me. I bend down and whisper the next name into his ear. He retrieves a black pin, and I pick at my cuticles until the ugly business is over with.

The rejected bachelor curses and shoves his way off the platform. My insides are all torn up as I watch him leave. After the door slams shut, I release the breath I've been holding. My shoulders sag, and a feeling of ickiness swirls in my gut. How am I going to do that eight more times?

Obi lands on my arm once again, and I whisper the next two names with a smile on my face. He looks up at me with those judgey little eyes. "You can hold one pin in your beak and one in your claw," I mutter to the bird.

He squawks a complaint but does exactly as I ask. *How is that bird so smart?* Across the room, he lands on Flare's shoulder, dropping a pin in Fenix's palm on the way. The twins smirk, and then barrel down the platform, elbowing and pushing each other to get to me first.

Flare wins, and I'm not surprised. Fenix grumbles as he hovers behind his brother waiting his turn. Flare's big arms envelop me, pulling me into the fiery furnace that is his chest. He picks me up and twirls me around until I'm giggling breathlessly.

"Good choice, firecracker," he whispers into my ear, sending an onslaught of goose bumps over my bare arms.

Fenix clears his throat, and Flare finally releases me,

frowning at his twin. With a lopsided smile in my direction, he saunters over to the right side of the room to join Elrian.

Fenix quickly moves in, tugging me into a warm hug. Like Flare, being within Fenix's proximity is like sinking into a jacuzzi. "Thanks for picking me." He brushes his lips over my cheek, and my face heats up. "I can't wait to get to know you better, Kimmie."

I tighten my hold around his waist before I release him, and he joins his brother against the far wall.

With my heart soaring, I opt to hold onto the high, picking a few more golds and silvers. Fraser, Elijah and Klaus all get the infinity pins while Ryder and Gunnar get the cute cupids.

Something niggles at my gut when Ryder steps up, but the thought vanishes from my mind when his lips crash into mine. My breath catches as electricity shoots through my veins at his lips' assault. I stagger back, nearly tumbling off the platform, but his strong arms lace around my waist and keep me on my feet.

Holy smokes!

When he finally releases me, a smug smile graces his chiseled jaw. "Don't worry, little minx. I plan on being upgraded to gold real soon." He winks and marches to the left to join the other bachelor maybes.

The gold and silver pins are nearly gone, and I have no choice but to choose some of the no's. Three guys get the axe and guilt weighs me down as I watch them leave.

One of them, Bart, I think, waves his fist at the remaining bachelors and grumbles something I don't quite catch. Methyss shoots him a murderous glare, and he stalks out, slamming the door behind him.

I exhale a long breath, squeezing my fingers together. Six men are still standing. Only a few more to go.

The crow flaps his feathery wings and lands on Lucíano's

shoulder, dropping a gold pin into his open palm. He shoots me a devastating grin and appears by my side faster than humanly possible. As he leans in for a kiss, the front doors whip open.

Bart and one of the other guys I'd dismissed storm in and pummel Lucíano to the floor. I scream as their bodies crash onto the marble in a tangle of limbs.

"Filthy parasite!" One of them cries out.

A slew of curses follow, and I stagger back to avoid getting sucked into the fight. The slap of skin against bone reverberates across my eardrums, and I cringe as I huddle in a corner.

Large shadows race by in a blur and after a few panicked moments, the two men are dragged out of the atrium. A couple of the chosen bachelors attempt to move toward me, but Methyss puts his hand up, stopping them.

I try to force my legs to move, but they don't obey. I think I'm in shock. How did this happen?

A medic makes his way to Lucíano and helps him up. His beautiful face is torn and bloody, and I suck in a sharp breath as he walks by. The sharp tang of blood snaps me back to my senses. "Oh my stars, Lucíano! Are you okay?"

He gives me a tight smile and nods. "I'll be fine," he mutters through clenched teeth. "Don't worry about me. Most of the blood isn't mine." His voice sounds garbled like he's got a mouthful of marbles.

I place my hand over my heart, trying to coax the rapid pounding to slow.

Methyss appears at my side, cocking his head. "Shall we continue?"

"Right now? Lucíano was just attacked." I'm horrified by everyone's lack of concern and only now realize the cameras are still rolling.

"Cut!" Dax steps out from behind a wall as if appearing

from thin air. In all the craziness, I'd forgotten all about him and the crew. He takes my hand and squeezes. "Everything's fine, sweetheart. Lucíano is tougher than he looks."

"And those guys that attacked him?"

"They'll be taken care of appropriately. Don't you worry about that. Jealousy is bound to be an issue in games such as these." He turns to Methyss and claps him on the back. "Let's finish this."

I nod, pressing my lips together. I wish Cross were here. His absence is a constant sting in my chest. Methyss walks me back to the platform, and I glance at the remaining bachelors. Most of them are no's, and I'm not sure I have the stomach to finish this.

A pair of sky blue eyes catches mine, and a sense of calm rushes over me. Cillian. Soothing heat swirls through my insides, seeping into all the nervous nooks and crannies. I fix my gaze to his and smile, his piercing eyes filling me with peace. One more gold before the black.

I signal to Obi, and he alights on my shoulder. Whispering my instructions, he brings the remaining gold pin to Cillian.

When his powerful arms encircle me, I almost forget the fight and Lucíano's bloodied face. Almost.

"You won't be sorry you picked me." He kisses me on the cheek and runs his hands up and down my arms. I'm suddenly so relaxed, I may topple right into his embrace.

"I'm already not sorry," I mumble. My knees wobble, and I wonder if he'll catch me if I fall.

He winks, shooting me a gorgeous smile. "I told you it wouldn't be much of a competition." He swaggers over to the right side, and I can't help but ogle his butt in the fitted ivory suit.

Glancing back at the table, only black pins remain. My

shoulders sag, and I motion to Methyss, pointing at the tray. I want him to be prepared if anything goes down this time.

He nods, clearly understanding my unspoken words.

I whisper the last names to Obi, and the remaining bachelors are escorted out of the room by two beefy security guards.

CHAPTER 14

The sound of crinkling paper wakes me from an uneasy sleep. I roll over, and it takes me a second to recognize the guest bedroom. I miss the sparkly chandelier and sweeping views of the ocean, but this room isn't bad. It still has a decent-sized balcony and attached bathroom. Most importantly, it's not tainted with the grisly images of the decapitated unicorn head—which I'm still not entirely convinced was fake.

An uneasy feeling sinks to the pit of my stomach. Again, my mind flashes back to the policemen and their discussion about the supernaturals. With all the weird stuff that's been going on, Lupita would totally have blamed it on witches or something.

I shake my head, pushing the crazy thoughts to the back of my mind and stumble out of bed. A white envelope by the door catches my attention as I make my way to the bathroom. That must be what woke me up…

Picking it up, I scan through the pages. It's a schedule—apparently, the group dates begin today. Along with the agenda is a suggested script for conversation points for the date. I skim the cheesy dialog and cringe. *Ugh. I'm so not saying any of this stuff.* I'm about to crumple it up, when a yellow post-it note stuck to the back of the second to last page catches my eye.

In tiny, almost illegible writing, three words make my heart stop.

Leave or die.

I gasp, reeling back until I hit the edge of the bed. I stare at the scrawled black writing, reading it over and over again.

Two faint knocks at the door send my heart hammering against my ribs. "Just a second," I mumble as I try to pull myself together. I fold up the script and the note and shove it back into the envelope and hide it in the bottom dresser drawer. Leaning against the mahogany armoire, I steady my breathing. "Who is it?" I finally choke out.

"It's Cristian—Cross."

I sprint toward the door, whipping it open and jump into his arms. I don't even care how stupid I look or that I'm still in my skimpy pajamas.

"Whoa, Kimmie, are you okay?" He staggers back, and I cling onto him like a baby monkey.

Footsteps sound in the hallway, and he quickly strides into my room, shutting the door behind us. I wrap my arms tighter around his neck.

"You're trembling," he whispers. He runs his hands up and down my back, muttering soothingly. "Everything's going to be okay." After a few seconds, he pushes me out to arms' length, his warm hazel gaze raking over me. "You need to tell me what happened."

I reluctantly release him and sit on the edge of the bed. I don't know if I should tell him. I'm scared, but I also don't want to lose this job. I can't. I need the money more than anything—especially now that my dad's sick. Would Sheppard and Dax cancel *Hitched* if their star's life were threatened? I can't risk that. This could be another prank.

I inhale a slow breath and run a hand through my disheveled hair. "I'm fine. I'm sorry I freaked out on you like that."

Cross sits beside me and arches a brow. "That didn't seem like nothing. You look like you've seen a ghost. Please, tell me what's going on."

I shake my head and plaster a fake smile on my face. "It was a bad dream. I can't get the image of that mangled unicorn out of my head."

His expression softens, and he snakes his arm around my waist. I lean into him, propping my head against his shoulder. His comforting, fresh-laundry scent envelops me in a protective bubble, and I convince myself I can do this.

"Where have you been anyway?" I tilt my head up to face him. "I really needed a friend yesterday."

He grimaces, and I immediately regret my poor word choice. He scoots further away, placing some distance between us. "That's exactly why I had to stay away." He grunts and runs his hand over his face. "Shep noticed us getting close, and he's not happy. He's having me work on behind the scenes stuff, and Gary's going to cover filming. That's why I came by today to tell you we couldn't do *this* anymore."

I jump up as anger bubbles inside me. "This? You mean talk to each other and be friends?"

He shakes his head, pressing his lips together. "I told you—"

"That's not fair. We're not doing anything wrong."

Cross stands and paces the length of the room, eating up the distance in long angry strides. He finally stops and turns to me. "Maybe not, but I want to." He grabs the back of my neck, and his lips crash onto mine. They're soft and warm exactly like I'd imagined they would be. After a heated moment, I pull away.

I can't do this. I'm not *allowed* to do this.

His eyes meet mine, and the swell of emotions he's trying to bury flash across his dark irises. A piece of my heart shatters. "I'm sorry," I mumble. I can't deny that I feel something for Cross, but I'm also starting to feel things for the other contestants. I'm here to play the game, and I can't do anything to jeopardize that or the money I desperately need.

He erases the space I created between us and takes my hands. "Come away with me. Let's leave and never look back. You don't need this job—you can find another one."

I shake my head and stare down at the plush carpeting as a jolt of pain lances through my heart. I don't want to hurt him. I meet his stormy eyes, and my chest tightens. "This is my big break, Cristian. I can't give that up."

He releases my hands, his shoulders sagging. "Right. Not for some measly camera operator." He turns away, but I grab his arm before he can get far.

"Please, try to understand. There are promises I've made to my family and to myself. I need to help them and the money… it could change everything. If things were different—"

He shakes his head, clenching his lips together. "But they're not." He spins toward the exit, and I release him this time. Before he closes the door behind him, he whirls back. "Just be careful, Kimmie. Things aren't quite as they seem around here."

The door slams shut, and I sink down onto the bed. How is this day turning into such a nightmare?

TRIXIE FINISHES BRAIDING my hair and steps back. "Okay, done."

I stand and walk to the mirror to get a full-body view of her work. I'm in tight jeans, boots and a fitted pink button down. Somehow, Trixie manages to make me appear flawless even with this casual look. More than that, she's succeeded in making me forget all about that ominous note. I shoot her a smile. "You're really incredible. Any way I can take you home with me?"

She cocks her head. "Ask me again when this is over."

My heart skips a beat. When this is over, I could be engaged... Would I move in with my fiancé? Can I really imagine marrying one of the remaining fifteen guys?

Trixie snaps her fingers inches from my nose. "Earth to Kimmie, you still with us?"

"Yeah, sorry." I tug at the collar of my shirt, readjusting it. "Just nerves getting to me."

"You do know how to horseback ride, right?" She narrows her bright eyes at me.

"Of course I do." My Uncle Jimmy had a farm a few hours away from home, and I used to spend the summers helping out. He had a gorgeous palomino named Tawny that I rode almost every day. "Are these actual horses or *unicorns*?"

Her mouth twists before she covers it with a smile. "Yes, actual horses."

The image of the massive flying creatures I'd seen from my balcony a few times flits across my mind. "Hey Trixie, have you seen those huge flying birds around?" A nervous giggle slips out. "They kind of look like the unicorns from afar." I realize how insane I sound, but I have to ask.

Trixie's eyes cast down to the floor. "Um, nope. Never seen them, but there are all kinds of exotic and weird wildlife on the island." She grabs my arm and pulls me away from the mirror. "Come on, it's time. The guys are probably waiting for you downstairs."

Trixie releases me at the edge of the landing, and I proceed the rest of the way by myself. I barely notice the camera crew anymore. Or at least I tell myself that so I don't search for Cross in the shadows.

At the foot of the stairs, Colt, Aren, Elrian, Lucíano and Elijah form a semi-circle. They're all dressed similarly to me in jeans and boots, and man, do they look hot. Colt tips his cowboy hat at me as I descend the final step, holding his arm out. "May I?" Short auburn hair peeks out from under his hat, bringing out the cute freckles smattered across his nose and cheeks.

"Thank you." I weave my arm through his and let him lead me to the golf carts waiting in the driveway. The other guys follow behind us, a few of them grumbling about Colt hogging my attention.

Elijah, Lucíano and the lone cameraman take the first golf cart. And I can't help the pang of guilt that fills my chest as Lucíano gives me a lingering gaze. Dating so many guys is going to be tough.

Shaking it off, I climb into the back seat next to Colt while Aren and Elrian take the far back, forced to ride backwards. I get terrible motion sickness so I thank my lucky stars I didn't get stuck back there. Just my luck, I'd puke all over one of the guys.

"Good morning, Ms. Starr." A pair of eyes catches mine in the rearview mirror.

"Oh, hi, Memmo." It takes me a second to recognize the driver from when I first arrived. He shoots me a smile as he adjusts his sunglasses. "Please, call me Kimmie-Jayne."

"Will do."

Colt stretches, and his arm lands around my shoulders. A smile tugs at my lips, and I turn to face him. I haven't had much of a chance to talk to him so I'm glad he's making an effort. The guys in the back don't agree as a wave of annoyed mutters emanates from the rear.

"Aww, stifle it you two," says Colt. "I haven't had a second alone with the gal."

I ignore them and turn to the cute bachelor beside me. "So you're a veterinarian? Is that why you chose this date?"

He grins, his big white teeth kind of reminding me of a horse's—but in a good way. "I am. I've always loved animals, and now I can really make a difference. I have my own practice, and I volunteer at a non-profit clinic on weekends."

My heart melts just a little. He seems young to have already finished vet school and started his own practice. I try to recall what his bio said, but I can't remember his exact age.

Aren pokes his head between ours, and his lips curve into a wicked smile. "Tell her what your favorite animal is, Colt."

The cowboy rolls his eyes. "I don't have a favorite, man."

"Must be nice to not be tied to only one—to be able to pick and choose animals at will."

A low growl rumbles in Colt's throat, and my head spins toward the sound. His green eyes narrow, the pupils transforming to slender slits.

What the heck?

"Cool it, Aren." Elrian's hand closes around the blonde's shoulder, jerking him back in his seat. A sudden breeze picks up, lifting Colt's cowboy hat right off his head. It sails onto the ground, tumbling across the grass.

"Son of a—," Colt cuts himself off as he jumps from the moving vehicle.

"Memmo, stop!" I shout, and the golf cart grinds to a halt.

Aren chuckles in the back seat, and even Elrian seems amused. My eyes shoot daggers at both of them as I jump off and hurry after Colt. *Boys*!

By the time I reach him, he's bending down to pick up the

runaway hat. When he straightens, his eyes are back to normal, and I'm convinced I'm simply going crazy.

I stand on my tiptoes to get a better look, but a pair of normally shaped pupils stares back at me.

He quirks a brow. "Everything okay, Kimmie?"

"I was about to ask you the same thing."

He wraps an arm around my shoulder and ushers me back to the cart. "Everything's cool. The guys were just messing around, and I let it get to me." He squeezes my arm. "Sorry if our antics upset you. It's hard fighting with all these guys for your attention."

I glance up, and his cute smile warms my heart. I lean into him, enjoying the feel of his fingers caressing my arm.

As we near the cart, Memmo's anxious expression makes me think I may not be going crazy after all. There's something weird going on around here and no matter how attractive these guys are, I can't let it distract me from discovering what that is.

CHAPTER 15

The sweet chestnut mare nuzzles my hand, and I offer her another apple. She munches on it happily as the guys get acquainted with their mounts. "That's a good girl, Mindy," I murmur, patting her golden mane.

Lucíano is already struggling with his black steed. He rounds the mounting block for the third time, but as soon as the Spaniard attempts to jump on, the horse backs away. I suppress a giggle as he mutters a slew of Spanish curses. It reminds me of the day I met him and the trouble he had with the *unicorn*.

Elrian trots over drawing my gaze away from the tragically comic scene. He sits on his elegant white horse as if it were an extension of his own lithe limbs. "Ready?"

I nod and swing myself up onto the saddle, bypassing the mounting block all together.

Elrian's smile widens. "So you've ridden before?"

"Just a little." I dig my heels into Mindy's sides and steer her toward the cluster of horses. Elrian moves beside me as we walk to meet our guide, his lilac gaze heavy on me. Lush tropical forests surround us, the chirp of unfamiliar birds filling the air. It's so beautiful I completely forget about the ominous note and the guys' earlier scuffle.

"Everyone ready?" Our guide, Jensen, sits atop his mount, circling the others.

From the corner of my eye, I spot Lucíano finally on his horse. The creature's ears are pinned back and its eyes are wide, showing more white than normal. Somehow Lucíano manages to steer him toward the rest of the group.

"Okay now, this is the plan," our guide continues. "We'll follow the path up the hill to the waterfall, then we'll take a lunch break and you all can relax for a bit before heading home." He pauses and glances at Lucíano. "Everyone good?"

He mutters a yes as do the rest of us.

"All right then, let's go." Jensen takes the lead with the cameraman to his side, and the horses follow in single file.

Overhead a drone buzzes to life, mounted with a fancy hi-tech camera. I wondered how they'd film the outings with only one camera guy. I kick my horse forward to move up beside Lucíano. The tortured expression on his face is sucking the fun right out of this. "Hey, are you okay?"

He clenches the reins in his fists, and his body is so tense you could bounce a quarter off it. "I'm fine, amor. Thank you."

"It might help if you loosen your hands a little. You're too hard on his mouth." I lean over and pull the reins out of his hands, and notice a gaudy golden ring on Lucíano's middle finger. The deep red jewel encrusted in the center of the antique setting glistens in the sunlight, refracting the light like fireworks. I tear my gaze away from the beautiful stone and continue muttering to the frightened animal. I have no idea what has the horse so spooked. "Also, don't be so stiff. Relax."

"Easy for you to say." His dark eyes flicker with amusement. "You look like you were born on that dreadful beast."

I laugh, and it seems to put him and the horse more at ease. As my eyes roam over Lucíano's perfect face, the image of his bloodied form on the floor of the elimination ceremony flashes across my memory. "How do you not have any bruises from yesterday?"

"I told you, the majority of the blood wasn't mine. They got a few punches in but no major damage." He shrugs like it was no big deal. I thought he'd be black and blue for days.

I must be making my confused face because he shoots me a reassuring smile. "I'm fine. I promise. As long as this beast doesn't decide to throw me, I'll be quite happy."

"Why would you pick the horseback riding date if you don't like them?"

"Because I like you." His thick accent and the deep timbre of his voice send a thrill through my body. "I'm not particularly fond of the other activities either, and I thought I'd have more of a chance to steal your heart from the first date."

Somehow, I'm trapped in his piercing gaze. The blood in my veins heats up and warmth flushes my cheeks. Why do all of these guys have to be so dang good looking?

He finally releases his hold over me, taking in a deep breath. "Tell me, what do you really want, Kimmie?"

His question catches me off guard, and I stop to consider. The clip-clop of the horses' hooves over the dirt and the droning of insects fill the gap of silence. "I want to be a famous actress, but it isn't only about that. I also want to fall in love, be a wife, and a mother." As I say the words aloud I realize how contradictory they sound.

His expression darkens, his kissable lips turning down. "And what if children weren't a possibility?"

A massive rock sinks to the pit of my stomach. *Whoa, this*

conversation got heavy fast. "I don't know," I breathe out after a lengthy pause.

Tentatively, he releases one hand from the reins and stretches it out to meet mine. "I want to be as honest as I can from the start. I can see a future for us, but unfortunately that wouldn't include children." He swallows thickly, his Adam's apple bobbing. "I'm afraid it isn't possible for me."

I quickly nod because all the words are stuck at the back of my throat. My chest tightens at the depth of sorrow masked behind those dark eyes.

"I understand if you eliminate me now. I only thought it was right that I tell you."

I squeeze his hand, gazing up at his bottomless irises. "Thank you for being so upfront with me." I want to say more, but the sound of approaching hooves stops me.

"My turn." Elijah appears at my side with a huge grin, his electric blue hair whipping up in the breeze.

Lucíano grumbles a goodbye and kicks his horse forward to walk beside Colt. I watch him for a few seconds to make sure he's okay before turning to my new suitor.

"Did I interrupt something?" Elijah glances from me to Lucíano and back.

"No. It's fine, Elijah. I'm just worried he's going to fall off."

At that, he throws his head back in laughter. "That man scares the crap out of animals. And by the way, I prefer Eli. Only my mom calls me by my full name."

"Okay, Eli. And yeah, I noticed that too about Lucíano and animals. I wonder why…"

He opens his mouth to say something, but then snaps it shut as if reconsidering.

"What?"

He shakes his head, wisps of blue picking up in the breeze.

"Nothing. I don't want to talk about him anyway. I want to talk about you and me."

"Okay, so tell me about yourself. Like how did you end up with that color hair?"

The crease between his brows deepens and something unreadable flashes over his face. Then it's gone. "I was hoping to learn more about you. There's not much to tell on this end."

"Come on…"

He clucks his horse on and then turns to face me. "I'm from California—Laguna Beach actually. I grew up on the water, that's my passion. Name a watersport and I've done it. Correction—I'm awesome at it."

"So that's why the blue hair? For the ocean?" I don't miss the fact that he's avoided answering my question.

"Yup." He wraps his hair around his finger and twists it into a knot at the base of his neck.

"I see. And when we were at the pool the other day, you said bartending was only one of the things you did. What else?"

"A little of this and a little of that."

Cryptic much?

A sharp whistle jerks my attention to the front of the line. Our guide has stopped and is trying to get everyone's attention. "Okay guys, we're heading up the hill so I need everyone in single file."

The riders and horses readjust, and Eli is the last one to move. He shoots me a wink. "We'll have to continue this later."

"We better."

He motions for me to go first, and I steer Mindy behind Lucíano. His horse is behaving, which I'm grateful for. As his dark head bobs up and down in front of me, our conversation comes to mind.

Could I really pick him knowing I'd be giving up the chance at kids? I can't help but wonder why he can't have any.

My chest feels heavy. I'd always been a sucker for tall, dark and mysterious, and I am really starting to like him. We don't have many of them in Clarksville.

The terrain becomes steeper, and I sit forward in the saddle to help Mindy. I'd been so caught up in conversation with the guys that I'd totally missed the natural beauty surrounding us.

As we climb higher up, breathtaking views of the ocean fill my eye line. Thick copses of green trees and fragrant exotic flowering plants cover the landscape, a rainbow of colors flooding my senses.

The gurgle of rushing water grows louder as we reach the summit of the verdant hill. After a few more minutes, we reach a clearing and the waterfall appears. I can't help my mouth dropping open. It's truly magnificent.

I tilt my head back to get a better view of the aqua waters cascading down the rocky face of the peak. At the foot of the falls, sits a sparkling pool with water so blue it looks like it's been painted.

"It's incredible," I murmur under my breath.

Aren trots up to me, his long blonde ponytail bouncing behind him. "I hope you brought your bathing suit."

"Yup!" I'm wearing it underneath my clothes actually.

"Come on."

I follow Aren and the other guys to the foot of the lagoon and dismount. Though the temperature isn't scorching hot, a dip in the refreshing pool sounds heavenly right about now.

I tear my eyes away from the glittering azure waters and settle on the five gorgeous men undressing before me. Heat seeps up my neck as shirts and jeans are tossed to the ground, revealing bare, well-muscled torsos.

"Come on, Kimmie!" Aren yells before diving into the pool. The rest of the guys are right behind him, so I tear my gaze away from their half-naked bodies and begin to strip.

I make a mental note to thank Trixie for suggesting I wear the bathing suit underneath my clothes. Undressing in the bushes would not have been fun. A second later, I'm rocking my red bikini and leap into the lagoon to join the guys, all modesty forgotten.

CHAPTER 16

The last golden rays of sunlight filter between the thick groves of green trees surrounding us as we make our way back to the manor. A huge smile is plastered across my face, and I realize for the first time in days I'm actually relaxed. My wet hair is piled on top of my head in a messy bun and my bathing suit is still damp, but I couldn't care less. The lagoon was heavenly and hanging out with only five of the guys instead of the whole lot was much easier. I'd gotten a chance to talk to each of them and was finally getting to know them better.

I go over all the interactions of the afternoon to catalog them in my mind until I can jot down some notes back in my room. Lucíano was his usual charming self, his soulful eyes and deep conversation keeping me more than interested. Eli wasn't kidding about the water; he seemed to be more at home beneath the blue surface than on land. Aren and Colt kept me laughing all afternoon with their playful antics, just the thought brings a smile to my face. Then there's Elrian—he's the most difficult to read of the bunch. Most of the time he's cold and aloof, but when he thinks I'm not looking I catch his lilac eyes intent on me.

I draw in a breath of sultry air and still my racing thoughts. What's a girl to do with so many choices?

I have one week until the next elimination ceremony, and I don't want to be caught off guard like last time. My chest tightens at the thought of having to say goodbye to five more guys in the next round. I swing around in the saddle to sneak a glance at the five gorgeous men behind me, and my breath catches. There's nothing like a handsome guy on horseback.

The path narrows as the terrain slopes downward, and I grip the reins tighter. "Whoa, girl. Good, girl," I whisper. To my right is a jagged cliff overlooking the ocean, one I have no intention of tumbling down. Regardless of how beautiful the view may be on the descent.

Mindy tenses beneath my thighs and without looking up, I know Lucíano must be nearing. What is it about him that has these animals so freaked out?

Lucíano's intense gaze rolls over my skin as he approaches, nearly hot enough to fully dry my bathing suit. "Did you enjoy our date?"

"I did."

He inches closer, our horses nearly rubbing up against each other on the narrow footpath. "So did I." His eyes linger on my mouth, and my tongue sneaks out of its own accord to wet my lower lip. A low growl reverberates in his throat, and my pulse quickens.

From my peripheral vision, I notice his horse's eyes bulge at the sound and then his ears pin back. I open my mouth to shout a warning, but it's too late. The horse spooks, tearing the reins right out of Lucíano's hands. The animal bucks and takes off down the treacherous descent.

"Lucíano!" My mouth finally gets the words out, but he's

already a few horse-lengths in front of me. I spin around frantically waving my arms to get our guide's attention. He, the cameraman, and the other guys are a few yards behind us.

Crap!

I have to do something. I dig my heels into Mindy's flanks and take off after him. Squeezing her into a canter, branches whip by my face as the scene blurs around me. My mare rounds the bend, and I catch sight of Lucíano's runaway steed, barreling around another tight corner. His hands are flailing, and one foot swings free of the stirrup. My breath hitches as the animal's hooves almost lose purchase on the rocky terrain.

"Lucíano, pick up your reins!" My fingers tighten around mine to keep them from trembling. Behind me, the pounding of hooves draws closer, and a hint of hope flares in my chest. Maybe our guide, Jensen, can save him.

Another turn and Lucíano's horse only seems to be gaining speed. I curse under my breath as I dig my heels deeper. Ahead, the path makes a sharp turn to the right with nothing but a steep drop on the other side.

Lucíano's horse gallops toward it, throwing his head from side to side as if the devil himself has gotten into the beast. My heart leaps up my throat at the moment I realize he's not going to make the turn.

His horse must realize it too, and at the last second he lunges his forelegs out, skidding to a halt. My heart stops as all the air is sucked out of my lungs. In slow motion, I watch as Lucíano somersaults over the horse's head and disappears over the ledge.

"No!" A scream tears out of my throat as I race toward the edge of the cliff.

A part of my brain registers the shouts to stop behind me, but I'm too blinded with grief to listen. I'm nearly there. I spur my mare on, even though I meet with resistance.

A powerful gust of wind stops Mindy a few feet before the ground falls away. She whips her head back, and I'm thrown backward with her as we hit a wall of air. The sudden smack snaps me back to reality and I gasp, my eyes widening at how close I am to tumbling right over the cliff myself.

"Kimmie, are you all right?" Aren's horse grinds to a halt beside me, and he quickly dismounts. He reaches for my horse's reins and steadies her as sweat glistens from his brow.

"I'm fine, but Lucíano..." Hot tears prick my eyes, and I'm seconds away from a total meltdown. I slide off my horse and take a step toward the ledge, but Aren's arm snakes around my waist, holding me back.

"Don't," I snap. I need to see for myself. Maybe Lucíano survived somehow.

Aren's navy eyes darken to an impossible shade of deep blue. He slowly shakes his head, grimacing. "You don't want to see what's down there, Kimmie."

"I need to see." I squirm free of his grip long enough to catch a glimpse of a body strewn across a platform jutting out from the side of the hill. *Oh, God.* I choke on a sob as Aren's warm arms come around me, pulling me into his firm chest. His hand slowly moves up and down my back, muttering soothingly like I'm some wounded animal.

Lucíano's stupid horse stands along the pathway, pawing at the ground. Anger unfurls inside me as hot tears roll down my cheeks. Jensen never should've let Lucíano ride alone, and now a man is dead. I push free of Aren's arms to tell our guide just that, but he's nowhere in sight.

"Where's Jensen and the camera guy?" I choke out, finally noticing Elrian and Elijah standing right behind us.

The three men exchange guilty glances.

I slap my hands on my hips as I look around. "And where's

Colt?" I suddenly realize the drone is no longer buzzing overhead either. When did it stop filming?

Elrian finally speaks up. "They went further down the hill to see if they could find a safe path down to the precipice."

I nod, wringing my hands together to keep them from shaking. Ice runs through my veins, and my teeth begin to chatter. *Lucíano is dead.* How could this happen?

Elrian shoots Eli a sharp glare, and the man inclines his head.

"Come here, baby girl." Elijah coaxes me into his arms, but it feels wrong. How could I revel in the warmth of his embrace when Lucíano is down there—alone? A beautiful tune fills the air, and it takes me a second to realize it's coming from Eli. His lips move almost imperceptibly over my head, but the rhythmic vibrations of his chest give him away. My head begins to sway to the ethereal melody, my eyelids growing heavier. I tighten my grip around his waist as my knees wobble, and the edges of my vision blur.

My eyes snap open, and I jolt up. A pair of onyx eyes fills my vision, and I scream.

"It's okay, amor. You're safe."

I'm sure my eyes are bulging out of my head like a crazed cartoon character as they run over Lucíano's face. "Am I dead too?" There's no other rational explanation.

A low chuckle rumbles in his chest as he lifts his hand to caress my cheek. "No, amor. As I said, you are safe."

"Then are you a ghost?" His hand is tepid against my skin, but what other explanation is there? I grip his forearms needing to touch him to confirm he's real.

He shakes his head, sadness creeping into his dark eyes as he regards me. "I'm not a ghost. I'm right here with you."

My eyes scan the darkening surroundings. We're still on the edge of the hill, only a few yards from where he plummeted to his death. "But it can't be," I mutter. "I saw you fall. I saw your body..."

Our guide, Elijah, Elrian, Colt and Aren all appear at once. Colt steps forward with a rope coiled around his shoulder and reaches out a hand to help me to my feet as Lucíano backs off. "Lucíano's one lucky son of a gun. He landed on that platform a few yards down, and we were able to rescue him. The fall knocked the wind out of him and he'll have some bumps and bruises, but as you can see, he's fine." He glances at the guide and Aren who both nod in confirmation. "How are you holding up?"

I run my hand through my still-damp hair and draw in a shaky breath. "I guess I'm okay." I glance up at Lucíano. His clothes are dirty and torn up but there's not a scratch on him—just like after the fight.

Am I losing my mind?

"Come on, amor." Lucíano holds his hand out, and I hesitantly entwine my fingers through his. "I don't know about you, but I'm looking forward to a warm bed and a stiff drink."

He leads me down the path as darkness descends upon us. The horses are gone, and two golf carts wait at the bottom of the hill. Lucíano draws me into his side, and my body curves into his. A part of me is ecstatic he's alive, but I can no longer ignore the part that's screaming something is very wrong here.

CHAPTER 17

I push back the covers and sit up, darkness blanketing my room. I can't sleep. Every time I shut my eyes, the image of Lucíano flying over the ledge fills my mind and I want to scream. Glancing at the clock, a crazy idea begins to take shape. It's not even midnight yet—maybe I'm not the only one having trouble sleeping.

Creeping down the quiet hallway, each rapid thump of my heart makes me wince. I reach the landing at the top of the stairs and stop about halfway across. The arched doorway leading to the guys' wing is closed, but is it locked?

I chew on my lower lip as I dance around in place. Maybe I should go back. The soft shuffle of approaching footsteps draws me closer to the door. I take a step toward it and jiggle the handle. The door pops open, and a dark figure fills the entryway.

"I thought I heard you out here, amor." Lucíano's lopsided grin makes my heart sing. After the horrible images flashing through my mind for the past hour, I can't help but jump into his arms.

I squeeze him tighter to make sure he's real. "I'm so glad you're okay." Pressing my ear against his chest, the sound of his slow and steady heartbeat calms the frantic beating of my own. He's really alive. By some miracle, he survived the fall. Without a scratch.

My earlier suspicions bubble up and I pull away, standing back to get a better look at him.

"What's the matter?" He cocks his head.

I glance down the hall to see if we're alone. Light seeps through a few of the closed doors along the hallway. "Can we go somewhere private to talk?"

His dark brows knit together, but he nods and turns toward what I assume are the bedrooms. After taking only a step, he spins back around. "On second thought, the walls are pretty thin here." He takes my hand and leads me back toward the entryway. "I know just the place." His midnight eyes twinkle, and my throat tightens at the thought of those beautiful irises nearly extinguished forever.

Lucíano whisks me out the back door of the manor, the crashing waves of the ocean echoing across the pool deck. A full moon and hundreds of twinkling stars light up the sky, reflecting off the dark water.

"It's so beautiful out here," I whisper. Somehow I feel like the magic spell weaving around us will be broken if I speak too loudly.

He leads me toward the white sandy beach, his fingers tightly clenched around mine. The cool sand seeps between my toes, and it feels like walking on puffy clouds.

Lucíano stops and turns to me when we reach the shore, the sharp angles of his face illuminated by the moonlight in the most indescribably striking way. "You wanted to talk about something?"

I will my eyes away from his piercing gaze and focus on

what I want to say. Of course now not a single word comes to mind.

His hand finds its way to my cheek, and I lean into the gentle caress. The moonlight flickers across his golden ring, setting the red jewel ablaze. "Please, amor, you can talk to me about anything."

That deep voice does things to my insides, and I find myself squirming. *Focus, Kimmie-Jayne*! How do I ask him my question without sounding like I belong in the loony bin?

I clear my throat and steel my nerves, which requires me looking at his chin because his eyes are much too distracting. "How are you alive right now? Not only alive, but without a scratch on you after that fall *and* after getting beaten up by those guys?"

His gaze casts down, and I swear his jaw clenches before a blank mask slides over his face. "I was simply lucky." He shrugs and turns away from me.

He's lying. Every fiber of my being is sure of it. I may not know him well, but this I know for sure. Not once has Lucíano not been able to look me in the eye. It's that smoldering stare that I find most attractive about him.

"I'm sorry," he mutters, still staring at the ocean. "There are things that we are not allowed to speak of…"

"What things?"

He tilts his head skyward, and I follow his gaze to a tiny red light blinking in the distance.

What? A camera-drone? I squint to get a better look, but if there really is a camera filming, it's a super stealthy one.

"Even out here?" I whisper.

He nods, finally turning to face me. "I was hoping we'd be undetected, but alas I was mistaken. I wish I could tell you more, but I promise it won't be like this for much longer."

I fold my arms against my chest trying to digest his words. What is he keeping from me?

"I'm sorry," he mutters again. "I want to be honest with you, but…" He pauses, his lips twisting into a cute pout. "As soon as I can, I will tell you all there is to know about me."

"You'll tell me everything?"

A smile tugs on his full lips, and he inches closer. His spicy scent lingers in the air, like a drug beckoning me forward. "Yes, and then I'll tell you everything. We all will." He licks his lower lip, and I find myself wanting to do the same.

My head tips forward, and his hand winds around the back of my neck. My heart takes off as tiny shocks of electricity dance across my skin. His lips claim mine, soft and gentle at first. He pulls me closer so that my body is flush against his as a sexy growl vibrates in his chest. He angles my head, deepening the kiss and my toes curl. *Holy shnike's*!

Much too soon, he pulls away and it's like a bucket of cold water extinguishing the fire that had only begun to burn. Anxious eyes meet mine as I suck in a breath to stop panting.

"Was that okay?"

"Of course it was." I giggle. It was probably the best kiss of my life, and I'm left wanting so much more. Not that I'd had that many kisses to begin with but still… groundbreaking.

Something unreadable flashes across his dark eyes—regret? Guilt? I can't tell.

He pulls me into his arms once again and I nuzzle his chest, the scent exotic and inviting. "I don't want to move too quickly —not until I can be completely honest with you." His breath runs through my hair, sending a tingle down my spine.

I glance up at him, fixing my eyes on his. "When do you think that will be?"

He shrugs, running his hands up and down my arms. "Soon, mi amor. Soon."

~

THE TWIST. I smack myself for being so stupid as I pace the balcony. After watching so many reality TV shows, I should've known there had to be one. Now here I am playing a game that I'm not sure I can win.

Lucíano can't be the only guy keeping secrets—they must all be. Couple that with the fake severed unicorn head, the threatening note and all the other crazy stuff going on, and I'm about to go into full out panic mode.

How can I keep dating these guys knowing they're all lying about something? How stupid am I to think I might actually find *the one*?

"Are you coming back in here or what?" Trixie's voice filters through the glass door.

I grunt, not sure I can go through with today's group date after my enlightening midnight stroll with Lucíano.

Bash slides the door open and pokes his blue-mohawked head out. "You okay, little bug?"

"I guess," I whine and follow him back inside.

He points at the chair positioned in front of the mirror, and I obediently lower myself into it. "We heard about the incident on the horseback ride. I'm glad that fine specimen of a man is all right." He clucks his tongue. "That would've been a terrible waste."

Trixie moves beside me and squeezes my hand. "Is that why you're upset?"

I rotate in my seat to face her. "Do you guys know about the twist?"

Her eyes lower to the floor, and she fiddles with the round brush in her hand. I glance in the mirror, but Bash won't even meet my gaze. A boulder plummets to the pit of my stomach.

"Not you guys too?" I sink down in the chair. Out of

everyone here, my stylists are the two people I trust most. How could they be keeping something from me too?

Bash kneels in front of me, taking my hands in his. "We're really sorry, but it's an iron-clad clause in the contract."

Trixie nods quickly, gnawing on her lower lip. "If we let anything slip we're out."

Great. I was sure I could pry the truth out of these two, but if that meant losing them, I wouldn't risk it. Not having them here with me would be ten times worse than worrying about the impending twist.

"Come on now, little bug," says Bash. "Turn that frown upside down." He spins the chair toward him and pinches my cheeks. "Today's hair and makeup sesh will be quick since you'll be spending most of the day on the boat or in the water."

Trixie picks up her makeup kit and digs through the brushes and compacts. "Yup. We just have to get you camera ready for the upcoming sequence, but nothing crazy."

The mention of camera makes me think of Cross. A sharp pain lances through my chest. I hate how we left things. Besides how bad I feel about hurting him, I miss my friend. "Do you guys ever see Cross?"

"Not much lately." Bash clenches a makeup brush between his teeth as he talks. "Dax has him working behind the scenes mostly."

"Why?" Trixie throws me a conspiratorial grin.

I roll my eyes and consider not answering, but if not Trixie who else would I talk to about this stuff? "I miss him," I finally blurt.

Bash wags a slender finger at me. "Tsk, tsk, Kimmie-Jayne. You know you're not supposed to covet the crew." He throws his head back and laughs. "And why would you anyway with all of that glorious male meat roaming around this place."

I can't help but laugh at the ridiculous grin on his face. I'm so glad Bash and Trixie are here, or I would've bailed on day one.

"So… is there anyone else you've *connected with*?" The higher pitch in Trixie's voice as she says the words makes my cheeks heat.

"No!"

She shrugs, twirling my hair between her fingertips. "What? It wouldn't be the craziest thing ever. You know what happens on these reality TV shows. Sexy times are practically expected."

"It's only been a few days, and I'm dating like twenty guys." I throw my hands up. I'm not about to tell them that my ex-boyfriend, Bobby, is the one and only man I've ever been with —in all senses of the word. Even kissing Lucíano is a big deal to me.

"Okay, okay. No need to get huffy." Bash dabs some blush on my cheek and winks. "For when you stop blushing."

I punch him in the gut for that one. He bends over laughing, and I shoot him the evil eye.

"Fine then." Trixie finishes up with my hair and plants her petite frame in front of me. "Is there anyone that stands out? Or any ones?"

"Maybe." I still can't get Lucíano's scorching kiss out of my mind, but there's no way I'm telling them about that. Not yet anyway.

Bash joins Trixie in front of me, pressing his arms across his chest. "Spill, young lady. I see that little sparkle in your eye."

If I'm being honest, I can't keep a secret to save my life. Two seconds later, I give in. "Lucíano kissed me on the beach last night, and it was ah-mazing."

"Yes!" Bash pumps his fist in the air. "That Latino lover is umm, umm yummy."

"So that's your type?" Trixie quirks a brow, sweeping back pink bangs.

"I'm not really sure what my type is, but I felt a connection with him from the first day. And then after the cliff…"

Trixie nods with a knowing smile. "Totally makes sense. Nothing like a near death experience to get the juices flowing."

A quick knock at the door puts an end to our conversation. "Come in!" I shout.

Sam pokes her auburn head through the crack. "You almost ready?"

"She is!" Bash helps me to my feet and leads me to the door.

My white sundress barely reaches mid-thigh, and my pink push-up bikini top peeks out from the low neckline. I can't believe how comfortable I'm becoming at prancing around half-naked in front of the cameras. Not that I'd need to wear more clothing for a day of snorkeling, but still.

"Let's go then." Sam holds the door open for me, and I sneak through. Marching down the hallway, I send up a quick prayer that today's date doesn't involve any more near death experiences.

CHAPTER 18

The boat rocks back and forth, a slight breeze stirring my hair as I keep my eyes on the horizon. No seasickness yet thanks to some miracle pill Trixie snuck into my backpack. We're only a few miles off shore and our captain, Siris, is readying our gear for the snorkeling portion of the date. Later comes swimming with sharks and stingrays —*yippee*!

A chill skitters up my back. After the bad luck I've been having, I'm wondering if swimming with deadly sea creatures is such a good idea.

"Penny for your thoughts." Cillian squeezes in beside me taking a spot against the railing and bumping Easton out of the way. I know it's him before he reaches me because his rain-fresh scent catches on the breeze.

I plaster on what I hope is a convincing smile. "Just enjoying the beautiful views."

He lifts a skeptical golden brow.

Man, I need to work on my acting skills. "I guess I'm a little worried about the swimming with sharks thing."

Cillian wraps a muscled arm around my shoulders and draws me closer. "Don't worry, angel. I'll protect you." His bright blue eyes twinkle, and a smirk pulls at his lips. He's totally making fun of me.

I throw a quick punch to his stomach—which is like hitting a brick wall. "Don't make fun," I whine. "You weren't there yesterday. You didn't see what happened to Lucíano. It was the scariest thing I've ever experienced."

Cillian shrugs, keeping his eyes on the ocean, but his expression darkens. "He's a tough bastard. It'll take a lot more than a little fall to kill that guy." He catches me staring, and the mysterious look vanishes. "Anyway, we're swimming with nurse sharks and the stingrays all have their stingers removed. It'll be like spending a day with a bunch of kittens. And even if something does go wrong, no one's dying on my watch. Trust me."

I inhale a deep breath to calm my nerves. I want to believe Cillian, and a part of me does. Underneath the cocky, arrogant façade, there's something else. He makes me feel safe, and I can't figure out why.

"You guys ready?" Siris approaches the railing, where we're all hanging out. Besides Cillian and Easton, Ryder, Klaus and Gunnar round out our six-some. Plus the camera guy and the ever-present hovering drone.

"Let's do this." Ryder tugs off his shirt, a wicked grin splitting his lips. Black swirling tattoos snake up and down his arms, and I can't help but stare. The man is cut.

The rest of the guys strip down, and now I really can't tear my gaze away from their ripped abs and corded arms.

Ryder shoots me a sinful glance. "Are you coming with or just going to ogle us for the rest of the day?"

So conceited. My cheeks flame, heat rising from my neck and I lift my sundress over my head only to hide the redness.

He lets out a long whistle, and I immediately regret my decision as I peek out from under my dress in only my bikini. "Now that's what I'm talking about," he growls.

I roll my eyes and pray the heat lighting up my cheeks fades quickly.

A few minutes later, we're all suited up in snorkeling gear, and the captain leads us to the platform. "Okay, ladies and gents, just like we practiced."

One by one the guys jump into the water until only Easton and me remain.

He motions to the crystal blue water, his pale hazel eyes catching the light. "Ladies first."

It's the most he's said to me since day one. I pause, half avoiding the unknown below and half curious to spend a moment alone with this shy guy. Instead of jumping in, I lower myself to the edge of the platform and allow my legs to dangle off the side. After removing my diving mask and snorkel, I glance up at him and pat the empty spot to my side. "Come sit with me."

His light brows furrow, and he rubs the back of his neck. "Um, okay." He props his mask on the top of his shaved head and sits beside me.

The steady lap of the waves against the side of the boat fills the silence between us. A few yards away, snorkels poke out of the water as the guys swim around the reef.

"So…" I finally say when he doesn't take the initiative. "Do you like snorkeling?"

"It's okay."

I kick my finned-feet in the water. "Have you done it many times?"

"Just a few."

Maybe I should give up and join the rest of them. One more try. "I've never really been a fan. To be honest, I'd never even seen the ocean until I moved to L.A. two months ago. The lake isn't exactly what you'd call a snorkeling hot spot."

He nods, and his lips almost crack a smile.

Geez, this is like pulling teeth. "So where are you from?" I actually know the answer since I've meticulously studied all of the remaining guys' bios after the last elimination. I'm hoping if I ask an easy question, he'll open up.

"Arizona."

Somehow I thought his bio was wrong because there is no reason for him to be so pale coming from a sunny place like Arizona. "You don't get out much, huh?" I slap my hand over my mouth the second the words are out. *What is wrong with me?*

This time I get an actual smile—one that reflects all the way to his eyes. "No, not really. I tend to keep to myself."

Wow, more than a three-word answer. Point for Kimmie!

"So what made you decide to come on the show?"

He shrugs, his eyes intent on mine for the first time. "Maybe I'm tired of being alone."

A wave of water splashes over us, soaking us from head to toe and a sharp squeal bursts from my mouth. Wiping the water from my eyes and sweeping the hair out of my face, two heads emerge right in front of us.

Klaus and Gunnar wear matching pleased grins as they remove their snorkeling masks. "Are you going to come swim or what?" asks Klaus, tugging on my leg.

"You're all wet now so you might as well," adds Gunnar.

Rolling my eyes, I reposition my diving mask and snorkel and wave a quick goodbye to Easton. I jump in feet first, instead of backward like we're supposed to—*oops*. Gunnar and Klaus swim on either side of me, and I dip my head below the surface.

It's like a rainbow exploded underwater painting the marine life in the most brilliant colors I've ever seen. Schools of fish dart in and out of the coral reef in vivid oranges, yellows and blues. The reef itself is varying shades of magenta and neon pink. I'm so absorbed by the beautiful kaleidoscope of colors, I have to remind myself not to let my jaw drop and suck all the seawater in.

Each of the guys take turns escorting me around the reef, and I must admit it's a lot of fun. Even though I don't get to talk to any of them much, it's actually a really cool date.

The hour goes by quickly and before I know it, the captain sounds a horn.

It's time to meet the sharks.

I scramble back on the boat with the guys close behind me. Once we're all settled in, Siris turns the vessel further out to sea. My heart pounds against my ribs with every rise and fall of the waves.

Much too soon, Siris cuts the engine and turns to us with a creepy grin. "We're here." He shuffles to the back of the boat and reappears with a big white bucket. The sharp tang of fish cuts right through the salty air as he pries open the container.

Bleh. I plug my nose and try to breathe through my mouth.

"Everyone ready?"

A chorus of "Yeahs" rings out, all except me. My palms are sweaty, and I have zero desire to go anywhere near a shark.

Siris dips a ladle into the fishy soup and begins to pour bloody guts into the choppy water. A couple of the guys race over to the railing to get a better look. I clutch onto the nearest pole for dear life as the first dorsal fins pop up from beneath the surface.

A second later the *Jaws* song is playing on repeat in my head, and every inch of my skin is covered in goose bumps. At least a dozen sharks stalk the boat, swimming in circles and snapping at the fish guts.

"Woohoo!" shouts Ryder as the feeding frenzy ramps up. All

of the guys are practically hanging off the bow trying to see over each other.

I've got a sweatshirt wrapped tightly around myself and zero intentions of going anywhere near those killers.

"Okay that's it," announces Siris. "Now we give them a few minutes to settle down and then you can go in."

Seriously? Whose idea is this? Get the sharks all riled up with a fishy appetizer and then throw in some humans as the main course?

I cling to the cold metal pole and sink down to the deck.

"Aw, Kimmie, you're not scared are you?" Ryder crouches down next to me.

I shoot him the death eyes and clench my fingers tighter around the pole. Every time he's around I get the strangest sensation in my gut—like there's something important I'm missing. I shove the thought away because dealing with the man-eaters in the water is more than enough.

"So you're really not going to come with us?" His lips turn into an adorable pout, and I hate him a little bit less.

I quickly shake my head. "I'll just watch from up here."

"Come on now." He reaches for me, but Cillian appears and smacks his hand away.

"Don't touch her," Cillian hisses through clenched teeth, his blue eyes an electrical storm.

A growl, one that sounds more animal than human, vibrates in Ryder's throat and bright yellow flashes across his irises.

What the—? I know I didn't imagine that.

Ryder turns back to me and forces a smile, his eyes black once again. "If you change your mind, I'll be over there." He jerks his thumb toward the circling sharks, and a pit sinks to the bottom of my stomach.

A second later, a loud splash makes me jump. Oh, please

don't let anyone get eaten today. Ryder might freak me out a little, but I still don't want him to die. I spin back to Cillian. "What the heck was that?"

He shoots me an angelic smile, flashing a dimple I'd never noticed before. "What was what?" He shrugs off my question nonchalantly.

Grabbing him by the bicep—*firm bicep,* I force him to look at me. "Why'd you get so mad at Ryder a second ago? And what is up with his eyes?" Something about the weird flash of yellow is eerily familiar...

He frowns, and it bothers me how he can even make a scowl look hot. "Is it wrong for me not to want anyone else touching you?"

Liar. He's seen other guys touch me before and never reacted like that. And he totally avoided my second question. I cross my arms against my chest, giving him my best stink eye.

Before I can wiggle away, Cillian traps me against the railing, running his hands over my arms. His warmth seeps in through my thin sweatshirt, and the tightness in my chest vanishes. I'm weightless—like I'm floating on a cloud.

A gorgeous smile stretches across his handsome face, and Cillian is all I can see. "Are you sure you don't want to try swimming with the sharks? It's perfectly safe, I swear." He ticks his head toward the back of the boat where the other four guys casually float around the killer fish.

A flicker of anxiety swirls in my gut, but a squeeze from Cillian's hand chases it away.

"I'll be right beside you the whole time. I promise."

"Okay..." I peel off my sweatshirt and follow him to the edge of the platform. A gnawing sensation in my gut tells me I don't want to do this, but my feet trail behind Cillian regardless.

"Finally!" Ryder treads water a few feet away and gives me a reassuring smile.

I try not to focus on the dorsal fins circling the men and concentrate only on the sound of Cillian's soothing voice at my ear. He's muttering something, but I can't even understand the words under his breath.

Clutching onto Cillian's hand, we jump into the warm water. I stay within arm's reach of the platform, but after a few seconds I'm surprisingly okay. A small shark swims past without sparing me a second glance.

Wow. I'm swimming with sharks! Excitement shoots through my veins, replacing the fear I don't even remember feeling. I kick my finned-feet, daring to venture out a little further with Cillian by my side.

"Look down," he says.

I stick my head underwater, and my mouth nearly drops open. Luckily, I'm able to control myself before I swallow a mouthful of saltwater. At least a dozen sharks swim underneath me, lazily circling the depths.

Breaking the water, I suck in a breath. "That's incredible!"

All five guys surround me now, their hulking bodies forming a protective barrier. I can't believe I'm actually enjoying myself. Easton and Ryder move out further, and I tug on Cillian's hand to join them. We swim just below the surface as the sharks coast below us. Time has no meaning as we drift along in the peaceful silence.

Small colorful fish swim between the nurse sharks—apparently, even they know the predators don't pose a threat with full tummies. The sun's rays filter through the crystal clear waters creating the most shimmering blues. I float along, following the guys and sinking deeper into a state of bliss.

A sharp horn blares through the water, suddenly shattering the tranquility. Two more short honks and then a long one. I lift my head out of the water and meet Cillian's wide eyes. "What is it?"

"Don't panic, just hold onto me."

My heart jackhammers against my chest, and I begin to thrash. "Don't panic?" I try to remember the horn signals Siris had gone over, but I can't hear myself think over the roar of my heart across my eardrums. I scan the endless blue for the other guys, but my brain is too frazzled to focus.

Cillian's eyes dart toward the boat, which is at least ten yards away, then to a pair of fast-approaching dorsal fins. *Oh crap*! These are about twice the size of the ones we've been swimming with for the past half-hour. Ice rushes through my veins, constricting my lungs. The serene blue blurs around me, my eyes fixed on the fast-approaching fins.

"Go now!" Cillian pulls me forward, his legs kicking like mad. I try to keep up, but he's so much faster than me. My arms and legs flail, splashing across the waves without making much progress.

Frantic shouts filter through the sound of the rushing water and my pounding heart. *We are so dead.*

Cillian stops, encircles his arms around my waist and lifts me from the water. I'm suddenly weightless again. "Close your eyes," he commands and for some reason I do. My eyes squeeze shut even though it's the last thing I should be doing with two killer sharks on our tail.

A warm breeze envelops me in its embrace, and a split-second later my feet land on the wooden deck. My eyes snap open as I take in the semi-circle of eyes glued to me.

"Are you okay?" Klaus's warm amber gaze is the first to fill my vision. Although, I'm fairly certain I'm still clutching Cillian's hand.

"What the heck happened?" I stutter. I feel numb, a weird haze lingering in my brain.

Siris approaches grimacing. "I'm so sorry, Ms. Kimmie-Jayne. Those tiger sharks never should've been out here." He bends to meet my gaze. "In all my years doing these tours, I've never encountered one, let alone two."

I gulp. Tiger sharks—the most deadly ones in the ocean.

"We almost got eaten by sharks..." I turn to Cillian, my head still foggy. "How did you get us back here so quick?"

He shakes his head, avoiding my eyes. "I guess it was adrenaline or something."

"But it felt like we... flew." I press my palms to my temples, trying to clear the haze to no avail.

Gunnar slaps Cillian on the shoulder. "He's a world-class swimmer, this guy."

Cillian glances at me sheepishly before diverting his gaze.

There is no way he swam us back to the boat that fast. My knees wobble, and I'm not sure how much longer I can stand. Now that the adrenaline is wearing off, my body weighs a ton. As if reading my mind, Gunnar wraps his arm around my waist and helps me to a bench.

Cillian takes the seat beside me and whispers in my ear, "You're safe now, Kimmie-Jayne. I won't ever let anything happen to you. Just rest now." Snuggled between the two big men, I let out a breath and lean my head against the railing. I'm safe now.

CHAPTER 19

A light knock at the door sends my heart climbing up my throat. I drop the book I'm reading and tighten the strap around my pink robe. After the hot shower, I thought I was feeling better but apparently my frazzled nerves don't agree. Opening the door a crack, a pair of sky-blue eyes peer down at me through the slit.

"I come bearing food," says a silky voice that immediately lights a fire in my core.

I open the door all the way, and Cillian strolls in with a takeout bag. His bright eyes scan my room for a second before returning to meet my gaze. "Your room is so much nicer than the shoeboxes they've got us in." He holds up the white bag and smiles. "Since you skipped dinner, I thought you might be hungry."

My stomach growls as soon as he opens the container and the sweet, garlicky scent of Chinese food fills the air. "Yeah, maybe I'm a little hungry." I snatch the bag and begin to unpack the containers on my desk. There's enough food to feed five of me. "Are you going to have some?" I feel silly stuffing my face while he just sits and watches.

"Sure." He smiles and pulls a chair up next to mine so we're sharing the small desk. "I wanted to make sure you were okay."

I swallow a big mouthful of shrimp lo-mein and meet his concerned gaze. "I'm still a little shaken up, but I'm hanging in."

His hand takes my free one, and he gives it a firm squeeze. Warmth pulsates across my skin, rushing through my veins. A sigh escapes my lips, and my whole body relaxes.

"Do you have some sort of secret power or something?" I breathe.

His impossibly blue eyes darken, and I swear he flinches. Then his expression returns to normal, and he shoots me a wink. "I can't spill all my secrets just yet."

I drop the chopsticks in the container, my appetite suddenly vanishing. Everyone here is keeping secrets from me, and it's making my blood boil.

Cillian clears his throat and scoots forward in the seat. "I'm sorry, angel. I wish I could say more, but big brother's always watching." His eyes dart over my shoulder, and I follow his line of sight to a blinking red light. The tiny camera is hidden on the bookshelf, concealed by two massive tomes.

How had I never noticed it before? When Dax said the cameras were always rolling, I didn't think that meant in my room too. I pull my robe tighter against me as an overwhelming feeling of ickiness makes my skin crawl.

Cillian must read my mind. "Don't worry, they're not filming you while you're showering or anything. It's motion-sensored and only turns on when there's someone else in the room with you. Didn't you read your contract?"

Good to know. No sexy times in the bedroom then. I start to shake my head, but he cuts me off.

"Dax didn't explain any of this to you?"

I narrow my eyes. "Nope." Apparently, there were a lot of things Dax, Cross and the execs conveniently left out.

He leans back in his chair, resting his hands behind his head, which makes his biceps bulge. "It's all about the ratings to these guys. They're probably hoping to catch you in a *scandalous* moment." He arches a sexy brow. "Want to give them a little show?"

I chuck an egg roll at his head, but he ducks, easily evading the fried projectile. It smashes onto the wall, leaving a greasy trail behind and I can't help the laugh that tumbles out.

"Now that's a nice sight to see." Cillian matches my smile with a breathtaking one of his own.

"Thanks for coming to check up on me."

"It's my pleasure." He leans forward and runs his thumb under my lower lip. It comes away greasy, and embarrassment rolls over me.

He did not just wipe my chin like I'm some messy toddler.

I grab a napkin and wipe my lips, resisting the urge to hide behind the thin white paper. "Thanks," I mutter.

A wicked grin lights up his face as he tucks his golden blonde hair behind his ears. "I'm glad I met you, Kimmie-Jayne. You definitely make things more interesting."

"Oh yeah, how so? You don't normally get attacked by tiger sharks on dates?"

He chuckles. "I don't usually go on dates so it's hard to say, but I can honestly admit you intrigue me. You're stronger than what I'd imagined."

I'm not sure if I should be flattered or insulted. Also why wouldn't he date much? I could only imagine the number of women who must throw themselves at him on a daily basis. His hand brushes my knee, and all my thoughts fly to the feel of his heated fingers on my skin. They slowly creep up my thigh until they reach the hem of my silk robe.

He sucks in a breath and snatches his hand back, tucking it under his armpit. I squirm, crossing my legs, abruptly cold from the lack of contact.

"Sorry," he mumbles, staring down at his folded arms. "After what happened today, I shouldn't be taking advantage—"

I cut him off, lifting a finger to his lips. "After what happened today, I could use a little distraction." Plus if I'm being honest, the afternoon's traumatic events have increased my attraction to Cillian tenfold. Saving my life earned the guy major bonus points.

And it is all part of the game, right? Kissing a bunch of hot guys is probably in the contract I never bothered to read.

I lean in, closing the space between us until our breaths mingle. Mine is coming hard and fast, and I hope he can't hear the erratic thundering of my heart. I wrap my arms around his neck and gently brush my lips against his. He drags my chair closer as he deepens the kiss, his hands exploring my lower back. A second later, he lifts me into his lap and I straddle him shamelessly.

Heat explodes in my core as the thin silky fabric of my robe presses against every inch of him. A moan escapes my lips, but it's swallowed up by his expert kisses. I tangle my fingers into the soft hair at the back of his neck as his tongue explores my mouth then moves down my neck.

This is getting more heated than I'd planned, but I don't want to think. I don't want to stop. I just want all the terrible things that have happened in the past few days to vanish from my thoughts—even for a little while.

I adjust my position and somehow my knee ends up a little too close to his family jewels. He winces and jerks up, his leg hitting the desk with such force that the drawer opens and crashes to the floor.

"I'm so sorry!"

He shakes his head, teeth tightly clenched. "It's okay," he hisses as I slide off his lap.

Ack! How could I be so clumsy?

"Here, let me fix that for you." He bends down to pick up the drawer, and the warning note I'd received slips to the floor. Before I can grab it, his eyes focus on the black writing.

I tug on the strap of my robe, cinching it tighter.

Fire lights up his bright blue eyes, fury dancing across his beautiful irises as he straightens and meets my anxious gaze. "Who sent you this?" he growls.

I shrug, pressing my lips into a thin line to hold myself together. "I don't know."

"When did you get it?" He crumples the note in his big hand, the crease between his brows deepening.

"Yesterday morning."

"Before Lucíano's incident?"

I nod, putting together what Cillian has obviously already figured out. "You think someone arranged those accidents?"

"I do now." He paces in front of my bed, anger blazing off him. "I can't believe Sheppard is still making you go through with this after receiving such a blatant threat."

I swallow hard, clearing my throat. "Well, actually… he doesn't know. No one does."

His eyes widen, the blue more bottomless than the ocean. "Are you out of your mind keeping this to yourself?"

Ouch. I twirl a lock of hair between my fingers, suddenly feeling very foolish. Risking my life to avoid losing this job seems a bit silly now. Lucíano could have died because of me. "I didn't think it was real." The excuse sounds hollow even to my own ears. "After the severed horse head, I thought it was just another prank."

He waves the note in front of me. "This is serious. We have to tell Dax and Sheppard about this immediately."

"Okay." I nod and turn for my closet. I can't go talk to the director and executive producer in this flimsy thing.

"I DON'T KNOW what you two are playing at, but this is not what I signed up for." Cillian looms over Dax and Sheppard with the note clutched in his fist. The sharp planes of his perfect face are contorted, fury radiating from his voice. He's terrifyingly beautiful.

"Calm down, Cillian." Dax rises from the couch in the entertainment area of my wing. Placing a hand on his shoulder, he speaks calmly. "I assure you that this has nothing to do with us."

"It isn't the twist?" I chime in from across the coffee table.

"Of course not," answers Sheppard. He unbuttons his jacket and slides to the edge of the cushion. "We would never threaten your life."

Cillian jabs a finger into Sheppard's chest. "Then you better find out who did. Or I'll take matters into my own hands."

The muscles in Cillian's back strain and bunch through his shirt. His shoulder blades look like they're going to pop right through the thin cotton.

"Don't you have cameras everywhere?" I ask. "Shouldn't you be able to see who slid the note under my door?"

Dax paces in front of the couch. "Didn't you say it was inside the day's itinerary?"

I nod.

Shep holds up his phone, showing me a series of text messages between Cross and him. "We already checked the footage. Sam dropped off the itinerary and no one touched it after that. There aren't any cameras in the crew area so there's no way to determine if anyone tampered with it before."

My throat tightens at the mention of his name. Now more than ever, I wish I could talk to Cross. It was stupid not to tell him about the note when I had the chance.

"So someone obviously put it in there before Sam delivered it." Dax runs his fingers through his spikey purple hair, tugging at the ends. "Don't worry, sweetheart, we'll have all of this sorted in no time." He crouches down beside me and takes my hands in his. "I won't let anyone harm a single hair on your pretty little head."

"And until you find out?" I have to ask, even though I'm sure I already know the answer.

"We continue as scheduled," confirms Shep.

At least Dax has the decency to look ashamed, his deep lavender irises casting down at the floor.

"We'll post security at your door twenty-four hours a day." Shep's cool gaze meets mine. "Welcome to stardom, Ms. Starr. It's the price of fame unfortunately." With a goodbye nod, he and Dax disappear down the grand spiral staircase.

Cillian drops down beside me and rakes his hands through his hair, exhaling.

"Thanks for sticking up for me." I intertwine my fingers through his and soothing energy flows up my arm.

There are three things I'm now almost certain of:

1. Cillian has some sort of magical calming power
2. Supernaturals *do* exist
3. One of them is trying to kill me

CHAPTER 20

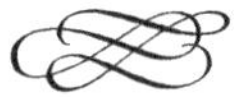

Sleep did not come easily last night, but the steady sound of the guard breathing outside my door did help a little. Now in the bright light of day, my chest doesn't feel quite so heavy. It's a good thing too because today is date number three—skydiving. With the intense weight pressing down on my shoulders, I'll probably sink like a rock and plummet to my death.

Who picked these activities anyway?

"How could you not tell us about that note?" Trixie's voice snaps me back to the present. She pulls my hair into a high ponytail and glares at me through the mirror.

"I don't know. I thought they'd cancel the show or something. I didn't want to lose this gig. I've got a lot riding on it." I don't feel like spilling the specifics about my families' money troubles to my new friends.

Bash rolls his eyes and slaps his hands on his hips. "Puh—lease, like Sheppard would lose all the money he's invested in this. No offense, little bug, but this show *will* go on."

"Unless someone kills me first." I wring my hands in my lap and snag my lip between my teeth.

"At least it'll make for exciting television." With a playful wink, he lets out a wicked laugh.

Trixie smacks his head with a wooden paddle brush, and I give her a high five. "I'm glad someone's on my side."

"I'm only playing with you, Kimmie-Jayne. You know I'd be crushed if anything happened to you." He places his hand on his chest, drawing in a dramatic breath.

"Whatever," I mutter. These two are my best friends here, and still they're hiding things from me.

Trixie's light brows knit, and she spins me around in the chair so I'm facing the two of them. "Nothing's going to happen to you, okay? And listen, today when you're out there, stick with Fenix or Flare no matter what. Do you understand?"

"Why?"

Her cute little lips turn into a pout. "I can't tell you. I'm sorry, but I need you to trust me."

My head bobs up and down.

"Like glue, you got me?" She squeezes my hand and unexpected emotion tightens my throat.

"I got it. Thank you."

SQUISHED BETWEEN THE hulking forms of Fenix and Flare in the sleek Cessna, I'm not sure which is louder—my hammering heart or the roaring engine. Every single nerve ending is on edge and even staring at Fraser's cute grin across the aisle isn't helping.

"Don't worry, lass, I'm wearing shorts under the kilt today."

In spite of the anxiety zipping through my veins, I crack a smile as my gaze falls to his lap. The image of the big Scotsman flying through the air with his junk hanging out is too funny not to.

"Relax," Fenix purrs in my ear, setting off a domino effect of goose bumps up and down my arms.

"I'm trying," I stutter.

Flare leans over and shoots me a megawatt grin. "After cliff falls and tiger sharks, skydiving should be a breeze."

I gulp hard. I can't shake the image of my parachute not opening and me plunging to the earth from my mind. "I'm really scared guys." I'm half-tempted to tell them about the threatening note, but I decide now might not be the best time. Nix and Logan sit on either side of Fraser across the narrow aisle, and I don't know either of them very well. I'm not sure I want to spill my guts yet.

"Don't be," says Fenix. "Skydiving is perfectly safe. Besides you'll have an instructor strapped onto you. Even if you don't know what to do, he'll take over."

"Have you guys done this before?"

The twins exchange a strange glance. Then Flare clears his throat and says, "Something very similar, but not quite this. Let's just say we spend a lot of time in the sky."

It occurs to me that I don't even know what these two guys do. Unless being drop dead gorgeous is there full-time occupation. I could totally see them as professional models. But maybe they're pilots? Too bad with this big secret everyone's hiding, no one will tell me the truth.

I chew on my lip, considering my next words. "Do you guys know Trixie?"

They both nod. "Yeah, sure. She comes and checks our hair and makeup before filming," answers Flare. "We're not this naturally good looking all the time." He smirks.

Another smile cracks my lips, slightly lightening the mood, and then I continue. "She told me to stick with you guys today.

She wouldn't say why, but she made it sound pretty important."

Fenix squeezes my hand and gives me a reassuring smile. "Don't worry. We got you. Cillian already warned us about your tendency toward accidents."

My palms are sweaty, and I'm sure he feels it. So embarrassing. I rub my hands against my jeans to get rid of the moisture. *Where's Cillian when I need that calming thing he does?* I draw in a quick breath and attempt to steady my racing heart.

"Okay guys, it's almost time," the pilot shouts over his shoulder.

The two instructors stand and one opens the door, and a rush of wind blasts into the cabin. "Who's first?"

No way in hell.

Fraser shoots me a smile and adjusts his pack. "I'll go first, lass, so you'll see there's nothing to worry about."

He blows me a kiss and leaps out the door like he's jumping into a backyard swimming pool.

I stare at the instructor without breathing until he gives the thumbs up that Fraser's parachute deployed. My lungs begin to work again, my heart returning to a somewhat normal pace. Nix and Logan line up next, and it occurs to me that I'm the only one that's jumping tandem.

That's odd since Flare said they'd never skydived before. I'll add it to my growing list of the unexplainable.

The other instructor, Max, staggers over to me, the wind impeding his forward motion and holds out his hand. "You're next, little lady."

My pulse skyrockets, and I'm sure my heart is trying to break out of my ribcage. "I—I..."

Flare shoots up, tightening the straps of his pack. "I'll go before her, then Fenix can go after," he informs the instructor. Then turning to me, he grips my chin between his big fingers.

"This way you'll be surrounded by us. It'll be like a Skyraider sandwich."

I try to say thank you, but the words stick to my throat. The inside of my mouth is like the Sahara. I squeeze Flare's hand as he steps to the edge and dives out headfirst.

My jaw drops.

"Do not do that," my tandem-partner warns as he tightens my harness and adjusts my helmet. The camera guy, Nick, is filming the entire thing so I stiffen my upper lip so I don't look like a total baby. Even though I'm fairly certain I may wet myself on the way down.

The other instructor waves us to the door, and I freeze. I will my legs to move forward but my feet are planted to the floor.

"I'll be right behind you, Kimmie." Fenix's warm voice cuts through the rising panic. "I promise I won't let anything happen to you." He sneaks a quick kiss on my cheek and blood rushes to my frozen extremities.

"Okay." I nod at Max, and we take the last few steps to the open door. Wind whips my hair across my face as I cling onto the handle by the door. One more step and we're flying. Or plummeting to our deaths.

"Whenever you're ready," the instructor shouts in my ear.

I hazard one last glance at Fenix and squeezing my eyes shut, I jump.

The floor falls away beneath me, and my stomach drops like a rock. My partner tilts our bodies so we're parallel to the ground below—or so I assume because I still haven't opened my eyes. The wind batters my body, the flap of my suit deafening across my ears.

"Open your eyes, Kimmie!" Max shouts.

"I can't!" My lips are plastered to my teeth as I try to talk. Then I remember the camera guy must be nearby, and I don't want to look like a total chicken. Slowly, I peek through the tiny slits under my eyelids.

As expected, Nick and his tandem-partner are only a few yards away. His helmet-mounted camera is pointed right at me. I squeeze out a smile but I must look terrifying with my lips sticking to my teeth.

I sneak a quick look down to the earth below us, and my breath hitches. The greens and blues of the island blur across my vision. Dark forms fly below us, and I'm pretty sure I recognize Flare as the closest one.

A bright red parachute shoots out from one of the forms, and I'm relieved whoever it is, is okay. One by one, a few others deploy and now only mine remains.

"Get ready to pull," he shouts.

I grip the metal ring and tug it down like we'd practiced. Nothing happens.

CHAPTER 21

The camera guy in front of me disappears as his yellow parachute engages, and he floats upward. My eyes follow him until my instructor's voice echoes in my ears.

"Try again. Harder."

Wrapping my fingers tighter around the ring, I jerk it downward. The cord snaps, and I'm left staring at the piece of metal between my fingertips.

Oh. My. God. "It broke!" The thunder of my pounding heart explodes across my eardrums as all the breath gets sucked right out of me.

"Don't panic," yells Max. "We've got an extra." He squirms around behind me, and I feel his arm shoot out as he engages the zip cord.

A slew of curses burst from his mouth a second later.

I struggle to turn my head to face him as ice crawls through my veins. "What happened?"

"I need you to stay calm, Kimmie." His face blanches, making it really hard for me to do that. "The second parachute is out, but we still have the back-up." He pauses and draws in a quick breath. "It's smaller than the others so we can't deploy it yet. We have to wait till we're closer."

"Isn't that dangerous?"

He grits his teeth. "It's the only option now."

Like hell it is. "Help! Help!" I start screaming like a madwoman, flailing my arms, and I don't care if this *is* going to be on television.

"It's no use—they can't hear us. It's too loud and they're too far away."

We're falling faster now, my stomach roiling as the ground approaches much too quickly. It's like I'm on a runaway roller-coaster with no end in sight—except the hard-packed, bone-crunching earth below.

"Help!" I glance up, and the bright blue of Fenix's parachute catches my eye. He's pretty high above us, but I swear his head tilts down. "Fenix, help!"

"Stop wiggling, Kimmie!" Max grabs my arms, restraining them against my body. "I'm going to try the last chute now." He pulls the cord, and I hold my breath.

The small white parachute pops out, and we're jerked upward. My pulse decelerates as we do, and my shoulders sag as relief rolls over me. "We're going to be okay," I mumble, mostly for my own benefit.

We float down to the earth, slowly at first. Then I feel it in my stomach—we're gaining speed again. The ground becomes clearer, small details springing to life too quickly. "Why are we going so fast?" I squeal.

"We're too heavy. The spare wasn't built to hold two."

Seriously?

My instructor begins to move behind me, swaying his body from left to right.

"What are you doing?" I crane my neck to face him.

"I'm trying to steer us toward the water. We'll have a better chance."

At not dying. That's what he didn't finish saying. Glancing up, Fenix's hulking body comes to view. He's closer now. "Fenix, help!" I shout again and this time I don't stop, despite my instructor's grumbling. Trixie told me to trust them, and I trust her. "Fenix!" I wave my arms back and forth.

Fenix's head tilts downward, and I think he sees me. It's hard to be sure with his goggles on. "Help!"

Max curses again, and I'm scared to look down. We're about to hit the ground.

Setting my gaze skyward, I plead for Fenix to hear me. His dark form seems to be moving, but I can't really tell from this distance. All of a sudden, his bright blue parachute detaches.

No! Not him too.

Tears blur my vision, and I choke on a sob. We're all going to die. I glance up at him one more time as a goodbye.

A pair of enormous golden wings shoots out of his back as a glimmering gold haze surrounds his body.

What the hell?

His massive body quadruples in size, his form contorting in mid-air. I squeeze my eyes shut because I'm certain I'm hallucinating. Maybe my life is flashing before my eyes. But I'm fairly certain I've never seen anything like this before.

An ear-splitting shriek echoes through the air, and my eyes snap open. An enormous golden dragon swoops down toward us, his leathery wings sparkling in the sunlight. He glides below us, extending his body and stretching out his wings.

Get on.

I whip my head from side to side at the familiar voice echoing in my mind. "Fenix?"

It's me. Trust me and get on the dragon.

I must be dead. This has to be heaven or hell or something.

Max is already swinging us toward the gigantic dragon so I

follow his lead. I climb on, clutching onto the golden scales on the creature's shoulder blades.

Hold on tight.

I flatten my body against the dragon's surprisingly warm skin, clenching my thighs and gripping so tight my knuckles are white. My instructor unlatches the harness connecting us and sits in front of me, his shoulders tense but the color has returned to his cheeks.

I'm riding a dragon... How is this real?

We glide the last few hundred feet and land in a clearing, where the rest of the guys are already waiting. The moment the dragon's talons touch the ground, I tumble off, landing in the grass in a less than graceful belly-flop. Hugging the dirt like a weirdo, I breathe in the earthy smell.

"Kimmie?" Flare crouches beside me and rubs my back. "Are you okay?"

No!

A large shadow blots out the sun as it moves over me, and I sneak a peek up at the immense golden dragon. A pair of smoldering amber eyes stares down at me.

I know those eyes. "Fenix?"

The creature snorts and two puffs of smoke shoot out of its nose. He sits back on his haunches, his long tail twitching.

My gaze bounces between Flare, the dragon and the rest of the guys. Only the dragon has the decency to meet my eyes.

"I take it this is the twist?"

A smile tugs at Flare's lip, and his emerald green eyes light up. He extends a hand to help me up and the hem of his shirt rides up, exposing the edge of his green dragon tattoo.

My mind flashes back to my poolside conversation with the twins. Fenix's dragon tattoo is gold, almost an exact replica of the humongous creature standing in front of me.

"Come on, lass, let's get you home." Fraser wraps a big arm

around my shoulders and leads me back to the awaiting golf carts.

No one has said a word to me yet, and my brain's been too busy trying to make sense of what happened to form a sentence. The fact that no one else even bats an eye at the twenty-foot dragon confirms my suspicions—not only do supernaturals exist, but I'm living smack dab in the middle of a whole house full of them.

Is that why I'm so drawn to each of these guys? I'm a helpless human unable to resist these gorgeous supernatural men?

The adrenaline fueling my muscles recedes, and anger ignites in my chest. I halt and spin back to face the rest of the guys, the cameraman and the skydiving instructors. "Is anyone going to tell me what's going on here?" I hiss.

Suddenly, everyone is much more interested in staring at their feet.

"Guys?"

The dragon stalks closer, lowering his head. My pulse quickens at its approach, but I force my feet to stay still. A golden shimmering mist blankets the animal, and its wings shrink, vanishing inside the big gold body. Then that too begins to contract, the long snout retracting, along with the thick legs and reptilian tail.

I blink and the dragon is gone, leaving in its place a very naked Fenix. My mouth forms a capital O as I take in his gloriously ripped body, and I drop my gaze. *Oh my*! Quickly realizing my mistake, I fix my eyes to the top of his head instead.

"I'm sorry I had to keep this from you." Fenix reaches out for my hand, but I retreat a step—and it's not just because he's butt-naked.

"So you're a dragon?" The words sound ridiculous on my lips. I turn to Flare, who's moved beside his brother. "And you are too?"

They both nod, matching anxious expressions on their handsome faces.

"Are they all dragons?" I tick my head at the rest of the silent bachelors.

"No," answers Fenix. It looks like he wants to say more, but he shuts his mouth and drops his gaze to the ground.

I swear I hear the cameraman, Nick, mutter a curse under his breath, but I can't be sure. "And what the heck are you?" I spin back to Fraser.

"My story is a long one to tell, lass." His mouth twists, and darkness settles over his features.

Nick steps forward—camera still rolling. He's got an earpiece dangling from his ear and a frown on his face. "Dax wants us to go back. He needs to talk to you about this in person." He passes by Fenix and shoots him a narrowed glare.

I remain rooted to the spot. I'm in no mood to go anywhere with these guys right now. I feel like the stupidest person alive. How did I not figure this out sooner?

Maybe because never for a minute did I really believe the rumors about the supernaturals were true.

Nix and Logan march past me, each giving me half-smiles before following the cameraman back to the carts. What kind of supernaturals are they? How many different types are there anyway? A million thoughts scramble through my mind as I wrap my arms tighter around myself.

Flare, Fenix and Fraser form a semi-circle around me, none of them moving. Finally, the Scotsman loosens his kilt and offers it to Fenix. "Put some clothes on, laddie. Don't you think the poor girl has had it hard enough today?"

I repress the chuckle threatening to break free with a hard swallow as Fenix accepts the plaid man-skirt, leaving Fraser wearing only his tight black boxer-briefs. I refuse to look at his muscled thighs. These guys aren't getting away with it that easily.

A part of me understands the lies were part of the game, but it doesn't help the sharp sting in my chest. I was just starting to get to know these men and open up to them, and now… It would be like starting over.

"I said, let's go!" Nick bellows from the golf cart.

I grunt dramatically and stalk over to the line of vehicles, choosing the one at the front. When Flare tries to get on with me, I shoot him a *don't you dare* look, and he takes the hint, joining his twin and Fraser in the second cart.

The drive back to the manor is a long one with all the crazy thoughts swirling in my mind. Was everyone I'd met so far supernatural? Trixie, Bash, even Cross? My stomach churns, soured by all the lies. I think back to my arrival, the fantasy ball, and all the outlandish things that have happened. Those really were flying unicorns!

Mind. Blown.

Can I really continue on this show, knowing that I could be engaged to a supernatural at the end?

CHAPTER 22

Dax and Sheppard stand shoulder to shoulder at the entrance of the manor as our golf cart rolls up the circular drive. Brilliant lavender swirls across Dax's pupils as I approach the steps, his enigmatic gaze raking over me. I should've known those eyes weren't human.

Throwing my hands on my hips, I shoot the two men a narrowed glare. "I almost died today." Saying the words aloud finally makes it all sink in. Seeing a real life dragon had temporarily distracted me from the terrifying truth. My hands tremble, and I clasp them together to stop the tremors.

Sheppard tugs at his shirt collar, and the lines across his forehead smooth. "I assure you, everything was under control."

Dax doesn't even look at me.

"It didn't seem that way from where I was. And how could you keep me in the dark about this? I like a good twist as much as the next girl, but this is unforgivable."

"I'm sorry, sweetheart—"

Shep snaps his hand up, cutting Dax off. "Ms. Starr, this is what you signed up for. It's regrettable that your agent wasn't clear with the expectations for this project, but if you're anticipating an apology for the twist you've come to the wrong place. I am of course appalled that you *could have* been injured."

I clench my teeth to keep my jaw from dropping open. Maybe I should've read that contract more carefully.

"This is a reality TV show, and our audience expects drama. Fair warning: there are more twists to come."

More twists? What could top a whole slew of supernatural bachelors?

My eyes bounce from Sheppard to Dax. At least he looks remorseful, casting his glowing gaze to the stone stairs.

Shuffling footsteps approach from behind, reminding me that the guys are still here. In my rage, I'd completely forgotten about them.

Shep ticks his head toward the five men now encircling me. "No one speak of what happened today. One of the crew will be in touch once we decide how to proceed. You may all return to your rooms now—except for you, Fenix."

Flare scowls as he passes by the E.P., a low growl vibrating in his throat. The rest of the guys walk by, only Fraser turns back to offer me a reassuring smile. He could keep that stupid grin to himself. Just like everything else they'd been keeping from me.

Fenix takes my side, his thick arms crossed over his chest. Shep and Dax exchange a few whispers before glancing in our direction.

"So now what?" I finally blurt.

"We'll look into the incident and move forward accordingly. Unfortunately, accidents do happen with these sorts of high risk activities." Sheppard's eyes ice-over as he regards the big guy beside me. "Pack your bags, Fenix. You're out."

"What?" I shout.

Fenix curses under his breath, the tendon in his jaw clenching. "But—"

"He saved my life." I try to keep my voice steady, but even I can hear it crack.

"While I'm thankful for that, he also breached his contract." Sheppard steps forward, a pretty brave move considering the look on the guy-who-can-turn-into-a-dragon's face. "It was rule number one: do not disclose your supernatural persona under any circumstances until allowed to do so."

Fury radiates from Fenix's bare torso, the air between us sizzling like a roaring fire. "You expected me to let her die?" he hisses.

The magnitude of his words hits me like a slap in the face. He's right. If he'd obeyed the terms of his contract, I'd be dead right now. My anger toward Fenix deflates, turning into warm fuzzies.

"We would've handled it," Sheppard retorts. "She was never in any real danger. I assure you."

"How?" I was there, and I'm certain I would have plummeted to my death if Fenix hadn't dragoned-out.

"Your instructor had everything under control, sweetheart."

I resist the urge to lunge at Dax and claw his beautiful lavender eyes out. I expect this from Shep but not from him. "You're wrong," I shriek. "Max didn't have anything under control. Unless he was some sort of magical creature and could've sprouted wings, we were both dead."

I search Dax and Sheppard's eyes and both refuse to meet mine.

"Max is human…" I breathe out. "Not supernatural." He couldn't have saved me.

Dax nods, clearing his throat. "But he's an excellent instructor, number one in his class. From what the cameraman, Nick, said, he'd turned you off course from land. You would've landed in the ocean and been fine."

Really? I didn't know much about skydiving or gravity if I was being honest, but even with the tiny toy parachute slowing us down, smacking into the water seemed like a risky idea. But probably would've made for super dramatic television.

"No, she wouldn't have," growls Fenix. "I waited, Dax. I saw that their chutes didn't deploy, and I waited for a while. Too long." He sticks his fingers through his hair, tugging at the ends. "I could hear her screaming." He shakes his head, his eyes glazing over. "It wasn't right."

I glance up at Fenix, the intensity brewing in his golden irises startling me. He'd been worried about me. I take his warm hand and entwine my fingers through his. I've completely forgiven the big dragon's lies at this point.

Shep's eyes are still frosty as they run over both of us. "While I appreciate your concern for Kimmie-Jayne, I repeat: she was never in any real danger. And it doesn't matter, Fenix. Rules are rules. You broke them, and now you're going home."

"Then I'm leaving too." The words are out of my mouth before I can stop them. Throwing my shoulders back, I steel my gaze at Shep.

"Sweetheart, you can't be serious." Dax makes a move toward me, but I recoil back, bumping into Fenix's bare chest.

"I'm dead serious." No pun intended. "I wouldn't be here right now if it weren't for him. He's probably the only one that actually cares about me, and I'm not letting him go home."

Shep rolls his eyes and grunts. "It's only a show, Ms. Starr. Don't delude yourself into believing anything more." His cold gaze settles over me, and he sneers. "If you breach your contract, you'll never work in Hollywood again. I'll make sure of it."

Dax taps Shep on the shoulder, and he releases his hold

over me. They whisper again, and no matter how hard I strain to listen I can't make out what they're saying. Do dragons have super hearing? I'm about to ask Fenix when Dax turns back to me.

"Kimmie, we really don't want to lose you. And honestly, we're under quite a tight schedule as well. Finding someone new would set us way back."

I throw my hands on my hips. "Well, you'll just have to do that. If Fenix leaves, then so do I. It's non-negotiable."

Shep mutters something in Dax's ear, and his brows knit. "If we let Fenix stay, we're setting a dangerous precedent."

I turn my glare to Shep. "You're the producer, I'm sure you can figure a way around it. Revealing what he is to save the star's life has to be worth something."

Dax smiles and whispers to Shep. The producer scowls and after a brief pause, nods. "Fine. We'll let Fenix stay," says Dax. "Can we move past this now?"

Why are they in such a hurry to produce *Hitched* anyway? There's something like desperation reflected in their eyes.

I snag my lower lip between my teeth as I consider. Besides standing in solidarity of Fenix's unfair termination, I'm not sure I *can* stay. I almost died… Then there's the whole supernatural thing. Could I really survive the next few weeks with a houseful of paranormal creatures? And then pick one to marry? Or at least pretend-marry? I shake my head, tossing the delusions of meeting *the one* right out. This is just a game—a reality TV show that could skyrocket my acting career and provide the money I desperately need. I have to suck it up.

"Yes. We can—I'll stay as long as he does."

Fenix's warm fingers tighten around mine, and a small smile pulls at the corner of his lips.

Dax nods also grinning.

"One more thing," says Shep, lifting a finger. "The twist

wasn't supposed to come out this soon. We'll need you to pretend you don't know anything until after the next elimination round."

Ugh. I'm tired of all the lies, but if this is the only way to get what I want, what other choice do I have?

"When's the next elimination?"

"In four days," says Dax.

"Fine," I grit out.

Shep nods and turns toward the door. His hand twists the knob, and then he turns back. "I hope your acting skills will prove on point when the twist is finally revealed. I need to believe it, Ms. Starr."

A-hole.

Dax follows behind him, mouthing a quick, "I'm sorry," before disappearing inside the manor.

I release the breath I've been holding the moment the door slams shut.

"You okay?" Fenix's thumb grazes my palm, moving in slow circles.

I sink down onto the steps, and he sits beside me. "I don't think I'll ever be okay again." The almost-dying thing took momentary precedence over the discovery that supernaturals exist and apparently walk amongst us. Now that I'm still in one piece, I have a whole lot to think about.

Fenix leans back, propping himself up on his elbows. "Well, I'm glad the truth is out. I didn't like lying to you or hiding what I am."

"And what is that exactly?"

"A dragon-shifter, of the great Skyraider pride. Beta to the leader of all dragons, my father."

My jaw pretty much comes unhinged. From my limited knowledge of pack animals, I assume beta is the second to the alpha which sounds like a big deal.

He chuckles and tosses a lock of dark hair back. "If you'd hear Flare say it, it sounds much more dramatic."

A small smile sneaks its way across my face. Flare definitely is the more flamboyant twin, but there's something about Fenix's unwavering steadiness that I'm really starting to like. Plus he saved my life so major points for that.

"Can you tell me more about yourself? About dragons—all of it?"

He ticks his head up at the camera above the entrance door. He lowers his voice and says, "Not here, but I know a place we can go." He stands and turns toward the house. "But first, I need clothes. I'll be right back."

I watch him disappear into the house, still trying to wrap my mind around the fact that Fenix is a *dragon*—an actual, honest to goodness, flying and fire-breathing dragon. And that's only him. What other supernatural creatures have I been living with for the past week?

A second later, Fenix is back, fully clothed and I'm wondering if super speed is a dragon-shifter ability. Taking my hand, he tugs me to my feet and ushers me down the driveway as the brilliant rays of sun dip into the ocean.

CHAPTER 23

The rocky cave juts out from the side of the hill with sprawling views of the darkening ocean. The rush of waves lapping onto the shore below fills me with a much-needed sense of calm. Fenix perches on the ledge, his gaze fixed on the sliver of moon peeking out between the clouds. The corded muscles in his shoulders are bunched as he scans the area below. I don't know how I didn't see it before—everything about his looming figure marks him a predator.

A chill skitters up my spine, and it isn't from the balmy breeze drifting over the ocean.

He stands and fixes his golden gaze on me, a shock of dark brown hair hanging over his forehead. "Looks like we're clear. I didn't see any of those buzzing buggers in the air." He sweeps the wayward locks back and moves closer.

My skin tingles at his ever-nearing proximity. I'm not sure if it's the *Speed* effect, but after such a close call with death *again,* I'm finding myself irresistibly drawn to the dragon shifter.

Dragon. My mind struggles to process the reality of the

word. This gorgeous man in front of me transforms into a fierce dragon at will.

"Are you okay?" Fenix's deep voice draws me from my inner musings.

"Yeah. I guess I'm still trying to wrap my head around all of this."

He extends his hand, his big fingers beckoning, and I gladly accept. After everything I've been through the last few days, I'm craving human touch. *Or not human, in this case.*

Fenix leads me further into the cave, and the gurgle of running water intensifies the deeper we go. "What's in here?" I ask as the light dims with each step I take.

"You'll see." He winks and draws me into his side. His eyes are practically glowing, and I wonder if his dragon powers give him super vision too.

The air thickens, warmth filling the cavern and chasing away the cold that had settled into my bones.

Fenix halts and pulls me to a stop next to him. "This is it."

I squint to try to make out anything but the inky black. "I can't see anything."

"Right, sorry." He chuckles and his hands come around my waist. He picks me up like I weigh no more than a ragdoll, pries off my sandals and sets me into a warm pool.

"Oh!" I can't help the squeak that slips out. The heated water feels heavenly, caressing my skin, the bubbles massaging my feet. I step farther in and the soothing warmth reaches my mid-thigh. My jean shorts are getting dangerously close to being soaked.

The crinkle of clothing being removed turns my head and a second later, Fenix splashes the water beside me. His skin emits as much heat as the bubbling spring, and I can practically feel him inch closer.

The darkness makes me bold, and I quickly tug my shirt

over my head and shimmy out of my shorts. Luckily, I'm wearing a matching set of cute black undergarments. A golden flame lights up Fenix's irises as he regards me, and my heartbeat accelerates.

Ducking into the water up to my chin, I inhale the mineral scent and throw my head back until I'm floating. A hand cradles my neck and another brushes my lower back, lifting me so I'm suspended just below the surface.

"This is heaven," I mutter.

"I'm glad you like it," Fenix answers, and I can hear the smile in his voice. He draws me closer into his chest, cradling me in his strong arms. "I figured you could use some relaxation after what you've been through."

Right. Reality comes crashing right back down on me, and the weightless sensation vanishes. Instead, I feel like a two-ton anchor sinking to the bottom of the ocean. The muscles in my back and neck strain, and Fenix must notice it.

"I just killed the mood, didn't I?"

I straighten, wiggling out of his hold. "I'm sorry, it's not you. I know I said I wanted you to tell me more about the supernatural, but for a minute, it was nice to forget about everything."

"So you want to forget, do you?" His hulking form looms over me, and anticipation uncoils in my gut. I can feel his head lowering, his warm breath dancing closer.

I tip my head up, my lips eager to meet his. As much as I want to know more about the supernatural world, right now the idea of getting lost in his lips seems much more appealing.

His mouth captures mine, and I willingly yield. His lips are smoldering, igniting a fiery volcano in my core. My body shamelessly presses against his, molding to his firm form. "Wow," I mumble and take a step back, afraid I'm about to be consumed in his fire.

"No kidding," he breathes against my lips.

"Is that heat a dragon thing?" I'm suddenly grateful of the darkness so he can't see the pink surely coating my cheeks.

"We do run a little hotter than most." He chuckles.

No kidding.

"Are you ready to hear more about us now?"

My brain says yes, but my raging hormones want to erase every inch of space between us. I suck in a breath and rein in my wild emotions. "Yes, I'm ready."

We sit on a ledge carved out from the rock, the warm water surging halfway up my chest. My eyes have gotten used to the dim lighting, and I notice Fenix regarding me with a lopsided smile. "Where do you want me to start?"

I try to organize the jumble of thoughts clamoring in my brain to form a complete sentence. "Okay, so you and Flare are dragon-shifter twins, and your dad is the alpha of your pack. So there are more dragon packs?"

"Prides, actually—like lions."

"Gotcha."

"Yes, there are dozens of other prides in Azar, but my father oversees all of them. Each of the respective alphas reports to him. They have a council, and it's all very civilized."

Two things stick out for me in that explanation so I go with the easier one first. "What's Azar?"

He holds his hands out. "This."

"This island? I thought we were somewhere in the South Pacific?"

"Technically, we're in another realm. Did you feel anything funny when you were in the airplane? Humans generally notice some sort of disturbance when crossing the ley lines that divide the human world from the supernatural."

My mind swims back to the flight and waking up to the

eerie blue light that bathed the cabin. "Yes. I did feel something. So you're telling me we're not on Earth anymore?"

Fenix throws his head back, and his whole chest rumbles with laughter. "We're not aliens, Kimmie. Our world exists parallel to yours, it's just hidden."

"And you can go back and forth as you please?"

He shakes his head. "Only certain supernaturals can open a portal to cross the barrier. A very powerful warlock will generally do the trick."

My mind spins from all this new information, but I try to remain open-minded before calling him out on total bullhonky. "Warlocks? As in male witches?"

"Don't let Dax hear you say that. Warlocks think they're far superior to witches."

"I knew Dax was one of them!"

He arches a dark brow, and his lips twist into an impossibly sexy pout.

"Sorry. That came out wrong." I trail my fingers across the gurgling surface and turn back to face him. "I can't believe Dax and Sheppard kidnapped me to another realm. That couldn't have been in the contract."

"It probably was—in teeny tiny writing. If Shep was involved, everything had to be by the book."

"What's Shep?"

"Oh, he's one of yours. One-hundred-percent human."

I balk. The executive producer of this crazy show is human... how is that possible? "So I don't get it. Is this show going to be broadcasted in Azar or in the human world?"

Fenix's wide shoulders lift almost meeting his ears. "That's the thing, no one really knows. TV shows aren't typically produced for us in Azar. We usually get the reruns from Hollywood. It doesn't make a lot of sense for Shep to waste his time on a supernatural production. It's kind of a big mystery."

The wheels grind in my head as I consider Shep and Dax's hurry to finish production of the show and their irrational concern over the twist coming out too soon. Could they be planning on releasing this to the human world?

"Do other humans know about you? Besides Shep?" I ask.

"Not many, but there are a few. Most of the crew is human —handpicked by either Shep or Dax."

"Is Cristian Cross human?"

The crease between his bushy brows deepens as he regards me. "The camera guy?"

"Yeah." I nod, keeping my eyes on the fizzing water.

"Yup." He makes a popping sound with the letter p and for some reason it's really cute coming from him. "He's worked with Dax for awhile now though. He's real familiar with the supes."

"Supes?"

He grins mischievously. "Yeah, you know, the big bad supernaturals."

Cross's betrayal stings. He knew all along, and he never said anything.

I abruptly remember the second part of my question from earlier. "You said your dad oversees all the dragons and you and Flare are his betas, right?"

He nods, the tendon in his jaw ticking.

"So when your dad retires, one of you will basically rule over all the other dragons? That sounds like a pretty big responsibility. And who decides between the two of you?"

His grin morphs into a scowl, and he grunts. "Yes, whoever is chosen will control the future for our entire species." He rakes his hand through his hair, and little droplets of water drip down his shoulders. "As for whether it will be Flare or me, that is yet to be determined."

The vein pulsing in his forehead tells me there's more to

the story than he's sharing. I open my mouth to ask more, but his arm snakes around my shoulders, drawing me into his side. "I don't want to talk about this anymore. If that's all right with you."

"Sure." The feel of his skin pressed against mine has turned my thoughts to other desires. I let him drop it for now, but I make a mental note to get more info out of Flare later.

There is something so warm and comforting about Fenix's presence. I can't wrap my mind around his two conflicting forms. He's more like a snuggly bear than a fire-breathing dragon.

"Thanks for bringing me here tonight." I nuzzle into his shoulder, his damp skin still hot beneath my cheek.

"Thank you for trusting me and allowing me to be frank with you." He tips my chin up and brushes his lips against mine.

"No, thank *you*," I groan into his mouth. Feeling feisty, I straddle the big dragon, a rush of excitement sparking in my veins. He responds with equal ferocity, and I lose track of everything but the feel of his fiery warmth pressed against me.

CHAPTER 24

The small two-story building sits at the very edge of the manor's complex, nestled between the wrought-iron gate and encroaching jungle. It catches my eye as Fenix and I walk hand in hand back to the main house, the first rays of sun kissing the top of my shoulders. Spending the night in the cave in the safety of Fenix's arms had been the best sleep I'd gotten since arriving on this crazy island. Somehow the walk of shame doesn't seem as bad with the big dragon beside me. I was hoping to get back to my room undetected but with the crew's quarters so close by, a new idea springs to mind.

I jerk my thumb toward the small motel-like structure—it seems out of place in the midst of all the lavishness surrounding it—and turn to Fenix. "I need to have a quick chat with Dax before the cameras start rolling."

"Okay, I'll see you back at the house later." His golden eyes sparkle, beckoning me toward him.

I get up on my tiptoes and he pulls me into his arms, searing my lips with a scorching kiss. I can't help but watch him as he saunters up the driveway, the muscles in his back and shoulders flexing against his tight t-shirt. Not to mention that butt—*holy dragon babies*! You could definitely bounce a quarter off that thing.

Turning back toward the beige building, I glance at my watch. It's nearly seven, and I hope I can find someone wandering about. Otherwise, I'll be banging at every door until I find Cristian Cross. That guy has some major explaining to do.

I'm not sure why I lied to Fenix about going to see him. The fib about Dax was out of my mouth before I could stop it.

A pang pierces my chest as images of my last encounter with Cross flood my mind. The look on his face nearly broke me. Now I'm wondering if I should've listened to him and left like he wanted. He was obviously trying to warn me of all this without actually saying the words. His contract must be iron-clad in regards to spilling the supernatural beans.

After circling the quiet building for the second time without running into a soul, I opt for a new plan. Taking the stairs to the second floor, I randomly choose the first door I come to. I send up a quick prayer that it isn't Sheppard or Tycen's room and lift my knuckle to the wood.

"Mornin', Ms. Kimmie-Jayne." A familiar voice sends my head spinning around, right before my knuckles make contact. My eyes land on the spiraling green tattoos up the short man's arms. Memmo—the driver that picked us up from the plane what seems like months ago. Now standing, his tiny stature becomes much more noticeable. He can't be more than four-feet tall. Could he be an elf or a dwarf or something? Do those creatures even exist?

I shove the errant thoughts to the back of my mind, reminding myself I'm not supposed to know about supernaturals yet and give him a big smile because he's looking at me funny. "Hi there, Memmo."

"Can I help you with anything, Miss?" His suspicious gaze bounces from me to the door I'm standing in front of.

I make a snap decision to trust him because besides knocking on every door I come across, I don't have a better option. "Yes, hopefully you can. I'm looking for Cross. I forgot which room he's in."

He nods, but his lips twist into a frown. He must be a stickler for the no-crew-and-talent-fraternization rules.

"It's important."

"Right this way." He motions down the hall, and the green vines roping down his arms shimmer.

Has to be a supe.

A moment later, he stops at a door. "This is it. I'm not sure if Cross is here though. He's been working on a special project for Shep the past few days—hasn't been around much."

A part of me is relieved at his words. I thought he'd been ignoring me on purpose, but maybe whatever he's been doing for the executive producer really has been the cause for his absence.

"Thanks, Memmo." I wait for him to leave before trying the door. I'm not a hundred-percent sure what Cross's reaction is going to be when he sees me, and I'd rather not have any witnesses.

Memmo waddles away and finally disappears around the corner. I inhale a deep breath and knock. After a few long seconds, the shuffle of approaching footsteps sends my heart galloping.

"Coming." Even muffled through the thick wood, I recognize Cross's voice and a horde of butterflies takes flight in my belly.

The door opens, and warm hazel eyes rake over me. My heart sputters, and I'm surprised by my body's reaction at seeing him.

"Kimmie," he rasps out, his eyes locked onto mine. "Is everything okay?"

Before I can stop them, my legs carry me forward and my arms lace around his neck. Tears prick my eyes as I inhale his fresh-laundry scent. "I missed you," I mumble into his shirt. I can't quite process what missing him means yet—whether it's only as a friend or more.

He backs away, holding me at arm's length and his eyes begin their careful inspection once again. "Are you hurt? What's the matter?"

I chew on my lower lip to keep the tears away, feeling stupid. I don't know where the rush of emotions is coming from, but I force myself to rein them in. "I'm sorry. Everything's fine. I just—I just wanted to see you."

Does he even know what's happened in the last few days?

Cross glances down the corridor and tugs me into his room. Folding his arms, he faces me, his lips pulling into a pout. "You know you're not supposed to be here."

I slump down on the bed and scan his room. It's small but clean with cream walls and generic framed landscapes. It reminds me of a highway motel, only a little nicer. Finally, I meet his gaze, the intensity illuminating his eyes startling. "I know I'm not, but after what happened yesterday I couldn't help it."

His light brows knit, and he crouches down in front of me. "What happened?"

"Well, I almost died skydiving out of a plane."

His eyes widen to the size of full moons. "What?"

"There's been weird stuff going on for days. After the unicorn head, I got this note and then Lucíano almost died, then the sharks and—"

Cross's finger brushes my lips, cutting me off. "You're going to have to start from the beginning because I have no idea what you're talking about. I've been off-property since I last saw you, and I just got back this morning."

"Oh." Drawing in a breath, I recount everything that's happened including the warning note I received.

When I finish, he moves to sit beside me and wraps an arm around my shoulders. I can't help but lean into him—his presence is so familiar and soothing. And human.

"You should have told me about the note," he finally says. "And I hate that you had to find out about the supernaturals that way. I'm so sorry all of this happened to you."

I suddenly remember I'm supposed to be mad at him for keeping secrets from me. Straightening, I shoot him my best dagger eyes. "How could you not tell me?"

He sighs and runs his hand through his short hair. "You know I couldn't. None of us could. You just told me how much trouble Fenix got into for breaking the rules, and he was doing it to save your life."

My mind flashes back to Cross's visit at Pollo Loco. It seems like years ago. The tortured expression on his face when he got the news from the casting director suddenly makes sense. "That's why you weren't happy I got the job?"

He nods, his lips pressed into a thin line.

"You knew everything, even back then." His betrayal pricks my heart. He was the one person I trusted here, and he'd lied to me all along. I shoot up to my feet and pace the length of the bed.

"So what are you going to do now?" he asks, his eyes following my every move.

My shoulders rise, nearly touching my ears. "I have no idea." I can't possibly tell him I'm starting to have feelings for these guys—supernatural or not, a few of them have gotten under my skin. The weirdest thing is how okay I feel about making out with multiple guys in less than a week. My sister would have a few choice words to call me right about now.

"Kimmie—"

Cross's voice pulls me away from thoughts of the gorgeous bachelors sneaking their way into my heart. I glance at the man in front of me, knowing he could easily have been one of them. But why did his betrayal hurt the most?

He steps closer but I maintain my distance, leaning against the armoire. "I'm sorry if I made things weird between us, because of what I did last time. I shouldn't have kissed you."

His eyes are on my mouth and though his lips are saying one thing, his heated gaze reveals another.

"I kissed Fenix," I blurt. As soon as the words are out, I wish I could take them back.

He jerks back as if I'd slapped him. Crimson coats his cheeks, and his mouth hangs open in a capital O. "What?"

As much as I hate hurting him, a weight has been lifted now that he knows the truth. "I'm finally starting to get to know the guys better with these group dates. You know why I came on the show..." I shrug, embarrassed to be talking to him about this. "They're all so normal and seem like really great guys."

"All? So you've kissed more than one?"

I wasn't planning on going into that much detail. My eyes cast down to the beige carpet, telling him what I'm too chicken to admit.

"Geez, Kimmie. I don't want to hear this stuff. It's bad enough for me to imagine what's going on." He digs his fingers through his hair and grunts. "Coming here was a bad idea." Catching my gaze, his eyes dart toward the door. "Maybe it's time for you to go."

My heart sinks to the bottom of my stomach. Wrapping my arms around myself to keep from falling apart, I turn toward the door. With one hand on the handle, I spin back. "I never meant to hurt you, Cristian. I'm just trying to figure out how to play the game."

"Well, you're getting pretty good at it." He turns heel and I do the same, racing to get out of his room before the tears spill over.

I make it halfway down the corridor, when a hand encircles my arm stopping me in my tracks. Spinning my head back, I meet fierce hazel irises.

"Just be careful, Kimmie. I won't be able to protect you from what's to come," Cross whispers, pain flashing across his expressive eyes. He stomps back to his room, and I'm left frozen and alone, ice crystallizing through my veins.

CHAPTER 25

I can't stop staring at Trixie and Bash as they swarm around me applying makeup and adding the finishing touches to my hair. Somehow Bash has managed to transform my pin-straight hair into wavy golden curls that would make Goldilocks jealous. I'm ninety-nine percent sure my stylists are supernatural, but I have no idea what kind. I should've asked Cross before he kicked me out.

A pang of guilt spears me in the chest as his tortured hazel eyes fill my vision. I hurt him again, and I'd keep hurting him as long as I remained on the show. As crazy as everything is, I'm not ready to give up yet. Besides the exorbitant amount of money and huge breakthrough for my acting career, I'm starting to feel something for these guys. The terrifying part is that I like more than one—maybe even more than a handful.

When did I become this two-timing vixen?

Trixie flashes her hand across my face. "Hello! Earth to Kimmie. You still with us?"

"Oh, sorry. Were you talking to me?"

"Only for the last five minutes," she snaps, rolling her eyes. "We're done. Do you want to see?"

"Yes!"

Bash whirls the chair around so I have a full view of my new look. Golden curls bounce on my shoulders, perfect spirals framing my face and spilling down my back. My skin looks flawless, glowing even. The light shimmery lip-gloss and dark eyeliner complete the cute but casual look, and I'm convinced more than ever that these two have some sort of magical powers.

"Thanks guys, I look great. You two are amazing."

Trixie wags her finger at me as I continue to stare at my reflection. "What's going on with you? You've been quiet all morning."

I swallow down the urge to spill the supernatural beans. No one knows about my near-death skydiving experience except for the five guys that were there, and they'd all been sworn to secrecy. I'm not sure that I'll be able to keep my end of the bargain for another four days—especially not from my friends. "I've got a lot on my mind," I finally answer, smoothing down my pink sundress.

"Too many boys and not enough time?" Bash winks and throws me a playful grin.

I can't help but chuckle—the guy cracks me up. "Yeah, something like that."

My stylists exchange conspiratorial glances and position themselves in front of me, blocking the mirror. "Tell us everything," says Trixie.

"Especially all the naughty details," adds Bash. "Our lives are so dull compared to yours. At least let us live vicariously through you."

"I don't think you guys know what you're getting into. Lately, I feel like I have a target on my back." My eyes flicker to the desk where I've been keeping the warning note. I may not be able to admit what I know about the supes, but maybe they'll have an idea about who sent it or what it means.

"Yesterday's date didn't go well?" Trixie's eyes dance mischievously. "Because word around the manor is that you didn't sleep in your room last night."

Bash gasps dramatically and throws his hand over his wide-open mouth. My cheeks flame, and a quick glance at my reflection confirms I'm as red as a ripe tomato from Uncle Jimmy's farm. "It's not what you think," I mutter. "Nothing happened."

"Well then you better tell us what did happen before we continue spreading the naughty rumors." Bash plops down on the loveseat and Trixie scoots in beside him.

"We're all ears," she says, sweeping her short pink hair behind her ears.

My eyes widen as they focus on the bejeweled pointy ends. "Your ears!" I shout and point like a crazy person.

"What are you talking about?" Her lips twist into a cute pout.

I march right up to her and reach for the pointy tip, but she slaps my hand away.

"You know!" Bash's squeaky voice betrays him as he jumps to his feet.

My mind is reeling as my gaze bounces back and forth between my two supposed friends. But how is this possible? I've seen Trixie's ears before and never noticed anything strange.

"The veil's been lifted," Trixie mumbles, more to herself than to us. "Who told you?"

What veil? I slump back down on the makeup chair and chew on my lip. Dax and Shep made it very clear I was supposed to keep my mouth shut until the big twist, but it isn't my fault I can see Trixie's weird ears.

"Just tell us how much you know, little bug." Bash crouches down beside me and squeezes my shoulders. "There's no point in hiding it anymore. You wouldn't be able to see through Trixie's glamour otherwise."

Throwing my hands in the air, I let out a long sigh. I'm about to spill everything when the blinking red light of the overhead camera catches my eye. Ticking my chin toward it, I shake my head slightly, hoping Bash understands.

He nods almost imperceptibly. Then his lips begin to move quickly, as if he's reciting a prayer under his breath. A minute later I glance up, and the blinking lights are off.

"Okay, we can talk now."

"What did you do?" I ask, scooting back in my seat. A part of me doesn't think Bash would ever hurt me, but the other part is too freaked out by everything that's happened in the past week to be sure.

"I turned off the power in the room. We don't have much time though. One of the techs will be here to check it out before long. Now tell us what you know."

I'm torn between wanting more answers about Bash's abilities and spilling all the pent up secrets. My chest feels like a dam that's about to burst.

"Okay, but it has to stay between us. Shep swore me to secrecy." They both nod, and I tell them everything that happened yesterday including my night in the cave with Fenix. Bash begs for the dirty details, but I insist nothing over PG-13 happened. I'm not a total floozy after all. Both of their faces grow grim as I finish.

"Someone really wants you off the show." Trixie folds her arms over her chest as she paces in front of me.

"Or dead," I murmur. These incidents are definitely escalating.

"But why would anyone want to kill her?" asks Bash. "It makes no sense."

It feels like the two-ton elephant that's been strapped to my shoulders for the past few days is gone. Being able to talk to my friends provides an immeasurable amount of relief. Maybe they can help me figure this out.

"Don't worry, Kimmie." Trixie pats my back and gives me a warm smile. "We'll find out who's behind this. If Dax and Shep are being pricks, we'll take care of it."

"But how? I'm not even supposed to know about any of it for another three days."

"We'll do some investigating on the down low," Bash answers.

"Thanks, you guys. I really appreciate your help." I clasp each of their hands and squeeze. With Cross wanting nothing to do with me, Bash and Trixie are the only ones here I can really trust. The guys are different—I still don't know if they have ulterior motives for being here. As much as I want to trust them, I'm just not sure. Shep already made it clear there may be more twists to come.

Bash's watch starts to buzz, and he releases my hand. "Ten minutes till show time."

I grunt, dreading the idea of another big group date. Handling fifteen human guys would be a hard enough task, but now knowing they are all supes adds a whole other level of anxiety. I'm going to spend the whole time trying to figure out what kind of paranormal creature I'm flirting with.

Bash and Trixie turn to leave, but I jump up to stop them before they get far. "Oh no, you guys aren't going anywhere until you come clean with me. What was that veil you were talking about and exactly what kind of supernaturals are you?"

Bash glances up at the camera on the wall, and I follow his

line of sight. Still off. He turns to Trixie and shrugs. "What's the harm now?"

She nods in agreement. "I'm a pixie, and he's a caster. And Dax veiled our non-human attributes to keep everything a secret."

I stare at the petite girl with the pointy ears and the blue-mohawked guy with a lop-sided grin, and I'm pretty sure my head is going to explode. "Come again, please?" I'm going to need a copy of *Supernaturals for Dummies* ASAP.

Bash glances at his watch again. "We don't have much time, but I promise we'll tell you more soon. Just know that we're both on your side, and we're going to do whatever we can to protect you, little bug."

Trixie wraps her slender arms around me. "You might only be human, but you're our human and we love you."

My throat tightens unexpectedly, and I swallow hard to keep the rising emotion at bay. Bash's arms encircle the two of us, and we remain in a comforting group hug until a knock at the door breaks us apart.

I sweep a finger under my eyes to make sure my eyeliner hasn't smudged and take a breath. "Come in."

Sam pokes her head in with a headset draped around her neck. "You ready? It's almost go-time."

I muster up a big smile. "Yup."

"Okay, let's do this." She ushers me down the hallway, and I push all the bad thoughts to a corner of my mind and lock them up tight.

The show must go on.

CHAPTER 26

The thundering buzz gets stronger the closer I get to the front door. I turn to Sam before reaching the foyer and arch a questioning brow.

"You'll see in a second," she says, her steady gaze not divulging a thing. I'm starting to hate surprises.

She opens the double doors, and strands of blonde hair whip across my face as I take in the four shiny helicopters idling in the front driveway. The fifteen guys are already onboard, and a few of them wave at me through the thick tinted glass.

"Have fun!" Sam's voice gets lost in the mad whirling winds and churning copter blades.

One of the pilots stands at the door of the helicopter and waves me over. *Here goes nothing.* A blazing ball of anxiety ignites in my gut as I imagine my fiery death at the hands of this sleek metal contraption. As I trudge toward the smiling captain, I send up a quick prayer that Fenix or Flare is in my aircraft. At least if we go down, one of them might be able to dragon-out and save us.

Stepping into the nearly all-glass cabin, my knees wobble with the engine's vibrations. Or maybe it's heart-stopping fear. The pilot hands me a pair of headsets as I quickly scan the interior, and my heart drops. No Fenix or Flare. Nix shoots up out of his seat by the window and offers it to me, scooting over to sit in the middle. He and Logan were with me at the skydiving incident and at least that gives me a hint of relief. They know that I know and though we've all been sworn to secrecy I hope they wouldn't hesitate to come out of the supernatural closet if necessary.

Gunnar, Easton, and Ryder round out the rest of the group, sitting across from me. I give them all the best smile I can muster as I buckle myself in.

"You're not going to be sick are you, Kimmie?" Ryder shoots me a wicked grin, and I repress the urge to punch him. Luckily for him, he's slightly beyond my reach now that I'm strapped in.

"Lay off her, man," Gunnar snarls, leaning over Easton to glare at him.

"Thanks," I mouth to the quiet blonde across the aisle. I haven't interacted with him much, but I remember him coming to my rescue after the unicorn incident too. My eyes roam over him, his words from that day taking on a whole new meaning now. He said he was a hunter—could he be some sort of paranormal hunter? Like a vampire slayer or something? His sinewy arm and leg muscles definitely look like they could do some damage.

The pilot spins around in his seat and gives us a thumbs up. "Everyone ready?" His voice comes in loud and clear through the headset.

We each shoot him a thumbs up in return, but my insides are churning faster than the helicopter's blades. The interior is nearly all glass, giving us three-hundred-and-sixty-degree views of the landscape as we ascend. The most clear turquoise-blue ocean and lush greens coalesce below us. If I weren't so freaked out, it would be beautiful.

Nix reaches over and takes my hand, giving it a squeeze. "Relax, Kimmie, you're safe with us." He ticks his head at Logan who sits on the other side of him. My eyes meet Logan's, and a flash of molten silver swirls deep within his irises. His flowing silver locks are a perfect match to his eyes. I can't tear my gaze away from their unique platinum hue.

Whatever he is, he must be able to fly or levitate or something. Nix's veiled message is clear and I relax a smidge, letting my tense shoulder blades lean against the back of the seat.

It's really too loud to talk to the guys now that we're higher up, and I'm actually relieved for the time to collect my thoughts. Gazing out the window, I take in the sprawling natural beauty below me. Azar. I still can't believe I'm in a whole other realm—one ruled by supernaturals. About a million questions whirl in my mind about this bizarre world I've been yanked into. Who rules Azar? Do they have a president? A king? I'd have to make a list of all my questions for next time I was alone with Trixie and Bash—assuming he could blast the electricity again.

What the heck is a caster anyway? A pixie I figure is like a fairy. No wonder Trixie reminded me of Tinkerbell when I first met her.

As my brain chews over all of these interesting revelations, my stomach drops, alerting me to our descent. I peer down in the direction we're heading and mossy green mountains stretch below us. One of the peaks towers over the others, and a plume of smoke billows over it.

It looks like we're heading right toward it. My eyes focus on the immense crag, and my heart drops as we grow closer. The mountain is not a mountain at all—it's a volcano. And from the looks of it, an active one. Fiery orange magma churns inside the crater as we soar above its mouth.

"You have got to be freakin' kidding me," I groan.

The guys are all peering through the windows now too, but unlike me, excitement fills their eyes.

At the edge of the volcano, suspended a few hundred feet above the crater sits an oversized tiki hut. A large wooden deck complete with a bar and various tables juts over the mouth of the volcano.

Logan leans over Nix and peers over my shoulder to get a better look. "Cool."

"You're crushing me, man," hisses Nix.

"So switch seats with me. I should be next to her anyway."

Nix opens his mouth to argue, but then snaps it shut at the last second as if reconsidering. He stands and gives up his seat to Logan.

The big silver-haired guy settles in beside me, his gaze locked on the scenery below.

I crane my neck back to face him. "Am I seeing things or is that a bar on top of that volcano?"

"Yup. That seems about right." He smirks and then undoubtedly notices my nauseated expression, and his smile falters. "It's probably an illusion," he whispers into my ear.

"The volcano?"

Logan nods, his silver eyes shimmering. "Could be. I've heard Dax is quite talented, and it is all about the shock-factor for ratings."

"So you don't know Dax well?"

"Nah. I don't spend much time here in Azar. My duties keep me in the human world most of the time." My mouth gapes at his willingness to discuss the supernatural. He cocks his head to the side at my shocked expression. "Fenix already filled me in on what he told you."

That's interesting. I hope he didn't fill him in on our heated moment in the cave. I want to take advantage of the loud surrounding noise to ask him more, but the pilot turns around, and his voice crackles through the headphones. "We're landing in two minutes. Everyone buckled in?"

They all shoot him a thumbs up but me, I'm too busy double-checking my restraints. The last thing I need is to fall out of the helicopter and plunge face first into a scorching volcano—illusion or not.

"Ms. Starr?" The pilot fixes his gaze on me.

Reluctantly, I nod and give him a thumbs up.

He turns back to the cockpit, and the helicopter pitches to the right. I bite down on my tongue to keep from screaming as the scenery goes topsy-turvy on me.

"I gotcha," says Logan, placing a rock-hard arm around my shoulders.

I lean into him, and it's like resting against the face of a cliff. All of these guys have firm chests, but Logan is different. There's no give to his torso whatsoever. I try not to think about it as the helicopter descends the last dozen yards and settles safely on a landing pad along the edge of the volcano.

The moment we touch the ground, I release a sharp breath.

Logan begins to unbuckle my seatbelt with a warm smile. "See, I told you we'd be all right."

Now that the helicopter blades have stopped spinning, it's too quiet to ask him anything more. "Thanks for putting up with my crazy."

He laughs, his steel eyes twinkling. "It's not crazy after what you've been through." He leans in closer and lowers his voice to a raspy whisper. "If Fenix didn't snatch you out of the sky the other day, I would have. Contract or no contract, no one's dying on my watch."

The intensity blazing across his irises makes my breath

hitch. I just stare at him for a few moments caught up in the power of his words. "Thank you," I finally mumble.

"You two getting out?" The pilot stands on the steps, offering me a hand.

I hadn't even noticed when the others had left. I take the man's hand and cautiously go down the steps. Not three yards in front of me sits the mouth of a gurgling volcano.

Logan takes my hand and leads me toward the tiki hut, staying well away from the edge. The tinkle of steel-kettle drums dances in the air as we climb up the stairs to the main deck. The fourteen other guys are already making themselves comfortable, most of them huddled around the bar.

"Come on. It looks like you could use a drink."

Amen, brother. I follow Logan to the bar, weaving in between the mass of thick bodies. "Oh, wait." I stop him before he reaches the bartender. "I'm technically not twenty-one yet." My big birthday isn't until next month.

"That's not a problem here. There's no legal drinking age in Azar."

Now that's a definite plus. "Great! I'll take a glass of champagne, please."

As soon as Logan's attention is diverted to the bartender, a crowd of guys encircles me. A couple of them begin to shoot off flirty comments, and I can't help but enjoy the attention. At least this will be a good distraction. Nothing like fifteen gorgeous men to take your mind off your problems.

CHAPTER 27

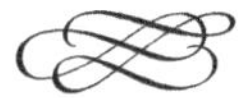

After the third glass of champagne, I'm having a hard time remembering my name let alone that someone's trying to kill me. Supernaturals, shmoopernaturals… I clink my flute against Lucíano's and attempt a flirty wink. He chuckles, and I'm thinking I didn't quite pull off flirtatious since I'm two sheets to the wind.

I've been making my rounds to each of the tables over the past hour hanging out with the guys, and as I sink into the lounge chair beside the dark Spaniard I'm feeling pretty good. He runs his finger down my arm inciting delicious sparks all over my skin.

"I'm so glad you didn't die." The words pop out of my mouth before my drunk brain can stop them.

He nearly chokes on his drink, sputtering. "I'm glad I'm still here too, amor."

I lean closer and breathe in his spicy Latin scent.

"Come on now," growls Fenix as he walks up. "It's enough we have to share you, don't make us watch too."

I spin around at the sound of his voice, the gravelly tone

making my insides clench. Fenix and Flare loom over the table wearing matching scowls.

"She gets friendly when she's been drinking." Ryder appears behind the dragon twins. He drills me with those impossibly black eyes and winks. "That's good information to know."

"Oh, stop." I stagger to my feet, holding onto the table for support. "Like you need alcohol to persuade me." My head spins as I force my eyes to focus on the three men in front of me.

Lucíano shoots up and grabs hold of my elbow. "Careful, amor."

I bat him off, moving toward the veranda. I want to get a closer look at the simmering volcano. Apparently, alcohol makes me flirty *and* stupid.

Elrian appears at my side, placing an icy hand on the small of my back, and I squirm under his touch. I can't quite figure him out. Like his touch, his personality borders on frigid. And yet, there's something about his enigmatic lilac gaze that draws me in.

We reach the wooden railing, and I stop about a foot away from the barrier. *Still not* that *stupid*. My eyes fix on the bubbling molten lava below, the heat warming the chilly air on top of the mountain. Can magical illusions emanate real heat?

I turn to Elrian wishing I could ask him. Keeping secrets is not my thing, especially not in my inebriated state.

"How have you been, Ms. Starr?" Elrian turns his frosty gaze to me as the wind whips up loose strands of white-blonde hair from its neat ponytail.

"Please call me, Kimmie-Jayne. Ms. Starr is so formal—" My words cut off as my eyes focus on his ears. His very pointy ears—just like Trixie's! I swallow down a gasp and quickly divert my widening eyes to the volcano.

Elrian's a pixie too? My hazy mind struggles to make sense

of this new revelation. He and Trixie don't seem alike at all, but I suppose that's pretty stereotypical of me to assume all pixies would be the same. That's like saying all humans are friendly.

"Are you all right?" His eyes find mine once again, and I can't help but get sucked in.

"Yeah, sorry." I sweep a lock of golden hair behind my ear. "It's been a pretty hectic few days."

A hint of a smile plays along his lips. "I'll bet it has."

I take a big gulp of champagne, finishing it off and set it on the railing. "Do you even like me?"

He doesn't even flinch. His gaze remains steady as he studies me, his inscrutable eyes moving over me with precision. "I'm here, am I not?"

That isn't exactly the answer I'm hoping for. Out of all the guys here, he seems the least interested in me. Whether the other contestants are only acting is beyond me, but he doesn't even try.

When I don't say anything else, he clears his throat. "I suppose the more important question is: do you like me?"

I chew on the question for a hot minute. "I'm not sure yet."

He dips his head and shoves his hands in his pockets. "I appreciate the honesty." It's the first time I've seen a fracture in his cold exterior, and I want to see more of that vulnerability.

A sharp crack cuts through the tense silence, and my knees wobble as the deck shudders beneath us. My hand shoots out to grab the railing as the champagne flute crashes to the floor. Glass sprays across the wooden planks then dances along the timber in tune with the tremors. Elrian's arms hitch around my waist, lifting me over the glass shards and into the shelter of his body.

The ground rumbles beneath us, and a wave of panic surges over me. I clutch onto Elrian's pristine button down shirt, pressing my body to his until the quake passes. Plumes of dark smoke lift over the railing shrouding the deck in a dense fog. Muffled shouts and the stomp of heavy footfalls fill the air.

"Everyone off the deck!" A voice I don't recognize sounds the alarm, and my building panic explodes into full-on terror. Fear hemorrhages through my veins, yanking me from the pleasant haze of alcohol. I'm dead sober now, and a scream builds in my throat.

Elrian scoops me into his arms and races across the platform. Whatever he is, he's super fast. People are running and screaming, practically trampling over each other to get to the helicopters. They must be humans—the thought scampers across my mind. My supernatural guys are all moving much more calmly. Except for Elrian. Are the others all impervious to boiling lava?

He sprints down the stairs, practically shoving people out of our way. The steady drone of the helicopter engines and swirling blades roar over the chaos. Just ahead, I spot Lucíano and Fraser. They part the crowd in front of them to let Elrian pass as I helplessly cling to his chest. He dashes toward the first helicopter with the pilot waving him on. I'm frozen, the neurons in my brain too numb to form actual thoughts.

Elrian gets me inside the chopper, and the pilot slams the door shut behind us. He remains outside, apparently waiting for something. I can't tear my eyes away from the mouth of the volcano only a few yards in front of us. The bright orange magma bubbles and hisses, shooting up into the air.

Dax suddenly appears out of the mass of bodies. His aviators sit askew on his head and he's shouting at the pilot, but it takes the man a second to register his words over the uproar.

"Go! Go! Go!" His cries filter through the chaos, reaching the pilot and me at the same time.

"Yes, sir!" He climbs into the cab and within seconds we're up in the air.

I don't even remember fastening my seatbelt, but somehow I'm all buckled in as the helicopter begins to ascend.

I hadn't even seen Dax at the bar all day. How did he get here so quickly? His tall lithe form gets smaller and smaller, and my chest tightens. *I hope he'll be okay.* I glance at the turmoil below as indistinct bodies swarm around the remaining helicopters. The volcano rumbles, sending tremors so powerful that I can actually see the earth moving beneath us. The fiery magma bubbles, spewing more red-hot liquid into the sky.

With my nose pressed to the window, I release a shuddering breath. "I hope everyone makes it out okay."

"Don't worry, they'll be fine."

I turn to face Elrian because there is something about his voice that doesn't sound right. His typically pale complexion is a few shades lighter as he stares out the window, his jaw slightly unhinged.

"What in the world happened back there?" I mumble.

His lips press into a grim line, his lavender eyes glossing over. "I have no idea."

So much for Logan's theory of the volcano being an illusion.

A brilliant purple light explodes below us, jerking my attention once again to the mouth of the volcano. A tall familiar figure stands atop the ledge with arms outstretched. The deep lilac glow bursts from his fingertips and settles over the sizzling peak. Throwing his hands out, he sends another flash of light zipping over the opening. His body sways from the ground-shaking quakes, and my breath hitches. *He's going to fall in.* After a few never-ending minutes, the earth ceases to shake, and the tremors no longer vibrate the air around us.

I point at the purple glow and infuse as much calm into my voice as possible. "Elrian, what is that?"

He shakes his head, a tendon twitching in his jaw. I can almost see the gears grinding in his brain. With a huff, he mumbles, "That's Dax trying to stop the volcano from erupting."

The conflicted expression on his face makes me momentarily forget my own panic. I turn to him, clasping his hands in mine. "I already know, Elrian," I whisper into his pointy ear. "I know you're all supernatural so don't worry about breaking your contract. I was sworn to secrecy but..." I shrug, letting the words fall away.

His mouth twists into a pout as his eyes rake over me. "You know, and you're still here?"

"Crazy, right?"

He smirks, and his lilac eyes light up. "I knew there was something I liked about you, human."

Why did the word human sound like an insult coming from his lips? "Thanks, I think." I sit back as the earth falls away, leaving behind the angry volcano and ensuing commotion. "Can Dax really stop it?"

He nods slowly. "Most likely, and if he can't, there are others with him who can."

Geez, these supes are insanely powerful. What kind of havoc could they inflict on the human world if they felt like it?

"So since I know now, can you tell me what you are?"

"I thought you said you were supposed to keep your knowledge of the supernatural world secret?"

I scowl at him, my brows knitting together. "What if I guess? I need something to get my mind off what happened."

"Maybe."

I can see his resolve falter, bringing a smile to my face. "You're a pixie, right?"

He snorts on a laugh. "Are you trying to insult me?"

"But your ears—" I reach for the sharp tips, curious to touch them since I first discovered them on Trixie.

He grunts and mutters a curse, sweeping his hair over the pointed appendages so they're hidden. "The veil *has* been lifted."

"That's what I just said." I cross my arms over my chest, pouting. "My stylist has ears like yours, and she's a pixie. So what are you then—an elf, a fairy?" I giggle under my breath until a pair of lavender eyes sear into mine. Their power scorches over me, branding me in their wake.

A shudder tattoos up my spine, making the hair on the back of my neck rise.

"I am Elrian Wintersbee, Prince of the Fae Winter Court, Ruler of the North, Master of Ice and Air." As he says the words, a tendril of icy breath curls from his lips, and I swear the cabin's temperature drops.

My mouth goes completely dry as Elrian's eyes spark with power. It exudes from his being and every ounce of me believes his words. He radiates royalty and authority.

He rolls his neck, setting off a domino of cracks. Inhaling a deep breath, he squares his body toward mine. "Much better. Keeping my powers veiled has been quite taxing."

The hairs on the back of my neck remain at attention, and I quickly scan the window to determine how far we are from the manor. Now that the veil's been lifted, there's something about him that has warning bells going off in my head. Of all the bachelors, Elrian seems like he could do the most damage. He's the freakin' prince of the fairies. Or Fae, I guess.

"Are you the one that's trying to kill me?" *Damn my loose drunken lips.*

The prince throws his head back and a deep laugh vibrates in his throat, actually reaching his lilac eyes. "Why would I want to kill you?" His expression softens, and he leans closer.

I scoot back, pressing myself up against the window.

He frowns, looking genuinely hurt and holds his hands up. "I swear on all the lives at Winter Court that I have no intention to hurt you." He pauses, watching my every move. "Why would anyone?"

"I don't know, but it's becoming pretty obvious that someone is." I unglue my back from the window and sit in my seat properly. Maybe it isn't Elrian, and it's just the leftover drunk brain that has me paranoid.

His light brows furrow, deepening the crease on the bridge of his sharp nose. "You're serious?"

My head bobs up and down quickly. "This volcano isn't the first time someone's tried to make my death look like an accident."

"The cliff with Lucíano?" He arches a brow.

"Yup. I almost fell over the edge trying to save him. Then there were the sharks, and skydiving with a no-show parachute."

He releases a sharp breath, shaking his head as he regards me. "Why would anyone want to harm *you*?"

"That's the million-dollar question."

CHAPTER 28

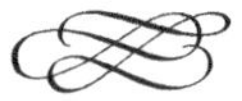

"Are you okay, firecracker?" Flare rushes into the sitting room where I'm curled up on the couch. I slowly nod and unwrap my fingers from the cup of tea I've been nursing for the last ten minutes.

It was excruciating—waiting without knowing if anyone had been hurt. As the big dragon pulls me into his chest, I realize I really care about these guys. Some more than others, sure, but if anything happened to them because of me... I nuzzle into the crook of his shoulder, allowing the intense scent of smoke and burnt wood to come over me.

Fenix appears on my other side and nudges his way in the middle, kicking Elrian off the couch. I watch as the proud fairy prince walks away without flinching.

I lean into Fenix's ear and whisper, "Did you know he's the prince of the Fae?"

Fenix *and Flare* both snort—apparently, I need to be more careful about my whispering.

"We're acquainted," Flare growls.

"So do dragons and Fae not like each other or something?"

The room begins to fill up with the remaining bachelors, and Fenix ticks his head toward the increasing crowd. "Supernaturals tend to stick with their own kind, but it's probably best to talk about this at another time as most of us have enhanced hearing."

Ugh. Only a few more days till the big supernatural twist, and I'm not sure I can wait much longer.

The front door slams, and the room goes silent. The sea of men parts, and Sheppard followed by Tycen and Dax stalk into the living room.

"Cut all the cameras now." Dax gives the order, and the barely perceptible constant hum halts. I hadn't even noticed the perpetual whirring sound until it was gone.

Shep and Tycen sit in the sofa across from me, while Dax prances back and forth, seeming too agitated to stop moving. I'm relieved to see he didn't get swallowed up by the angry volcano.

Shep sits forward, unbuttoning his elegant three-piece suit. "There are a few things we need to discuss."

"Damn right, you do," snarls Flare. A flash of emerald swirls in his eyes as his pupils elongate. "There is obviously something going on here, and we want to know what you're doing about it. Putting *our* lives at risk is one thing, but how about hers?" He fixes his unearthly gaze on Shep and Tycen. "We're a bit more durable, but you'd think you'd be more concerned in protecting one of your own."

Note to self: Shep and Tycen are both definitely human. And I'm totally digging Flare's protective vibe.

Sheppard doesn't balk. "Watch yourself, Skyraider. I permitted your brother to stay out of the kindness of my heart, but I'm not *that* kind."

Fenix sits forward now, steepling his fingers. "You know our father would not hesitate to withdraw his support from—"

Sheppard blanches and raises his hand, cutting off the rest of Fenix's words. "There's no need for that. I have everything under control."

"Do you really?" Cillian moves from behind the couch to glare at the execs. "Kimmie-Jayne's life has been threatened more times than I can count now. And if it weren't for us, I'm not certain she would have survived."

A chill skitters up my spine as I absorb his words. He's right. I'd be dead right now at least three times over if one of the supernatural bachelors hadn't intervened.

Sheppard stands and faces the whole group of us. "You all know there is a lot riding on this show."

I roll my eyes—it's only about ratings and advertising money to this guy. He doesn't care if I die in the process as long as it's caught on camera.

He must notice my dramatic eye roll because he turns his icy gaze to me. "I'm sorry I can't share more with you right now, but suffice it to say, there's more at stake here than just a television show."

What the heck does that mean?

He crouches in front of me and his expression softens, the hard set of his jaw yielding. I don't think I've ever seen that vulnerable look on the mighty Sheppard Hawk. "Please, Kimmie. I'm asking you to hold out only a few more days." He scans the gaggle of guys surrounding me. "You'll be safe with them for now."

Dax moves to the center of the semi-circle formed around the couch. "After some discussion, we've decided to move the next elimination round up. We're certain that once the twist has been revealed, the *accidents* will stop."

Accidents? More like attempted murders.

"Why would you think that?" asks Elrian.

Sheppard jumps in before Dax can get another word out.

"Because we believe that someone is trying to sabotage the big reveal. All of these strange occurrences are meant to stop us. But we're not going to let whoever is behind this win. Once the next elimination is filmed, it's done. There won't be anything anyone can do to stop *Hitched* from airing."

I try to fill in the blanks from his vague explanation with what I already know. The twist involves revealing that the bachelors are all supernatural. So why does someone not want that happening? Then I process Dax's earlier words, and panic surges in my gut. "Wait, when are you moving the elimination to?"

"Tomorrow."

~

How can I possibly choose?

I pace back and forth in front of the balcony with the bachelor bio sheet pressed against my chest. Having to send five guys home tomorrow is twisting my insides into the shape of a Twizzler.

There hasn't been enough time for me to really get to know a lot of them. And with all the death threats looming over me, it's been hard to concentrate on my love life. Images of steamy make-out sessions with Fenix, Cillian, and Lucíano flicker through my vision, and my gut clenches as a wave of warmth consumes me. Okay, so maybe I have made *some* time for fun.

I grab the pen sticking out of my messy bun and jot down a few more notes by the guys' pictures. Fenix, Cillian, and Lucíano are definitely staying. I'm looking forward to some more alone time with each of them.

Closing my eyes, I lean against the cool glass of the sliding door. Could I see myself engaged to one of them? I don't even know what kind of supernaturals Cillian and Lucíano are. And what about Fenix—if we do get married, does that mean we'll have dragon babies?

I giggle at the insanity of it all. Just a few weeks ago I was slinging chicken off a smoking grill, and now... Now I'm contemplating dragon babies. The thought of children reminds me of my heart-to-heart with Lucíano. I wonder if the reason he can't have kids has something to do with what he is.

I scan the page of gorgeous guys and sigh. It would be so much easier to choose if I knew who was what. Is that being racist though? I shake my head at the errant thought.

And did it really matter anyway? Isn't this just a step in my acting career? Running my hands through my hair, I shove away the conflicting thoughts. *You gotta get your priorities straight, Kimmie-Jayne*!

Two quiet knocks at my door send my heartbeats into overtime. Oh stars, what if someone's here to kill me... I creep toward the door on tiptoes and then stop about a foot away.

"I can hear you breathing." A familiar cutting voice seeps through the crack. "Plus your guard is still out here, and I don't think he'd let anyone dangerous in."

I take a step back and open the door. Elrian. Probably the last person I expected to show up at my room at this late hour.

"Hi." I run a hand through my hair again, sweeping the golden wisps back behind my ears.

"I hope I'm not disturbing you." He stands at the threshold, looking all the dignified, standoffish prince. Now that I know what he is, I don't know how I didn't see it before—not the Fae part, but the royalty part.

"No, of course not." I tuck the bio sheet into my desk drawer and motion for him to come in.

He sits stiffly on the love seat, and I fold into the chair across from him.

"So what's up?"

He crosses his legs and adjusts his position as if he's sitting on hot pokers. "I came to check on you. To make sure you were okay after what happened today. Since the elimination is tomorrow, I wasn't sure I'd get another chance." His mysterious lilac eyes cast down to the floor.

He's worried I'm not going to pick him. The revelation is both startling and flattering.

"Thank you," I say finally. "I'm doing okay, but definitely glad for some company."

The tight set of his jaw relaxes a smidge.

There are so many questions I want to ask him but have to keep my mouth shut as the blinking red light on the camera circles the space. The silence intensifies, and now I'm squirming in my seat. "Do you want something to drink? Aurelia made me a pot of tea to calm my nerves."

"I'd like that, thank you."

I bounce out of the chair and pour two steaming cups. As I approach, I catch Elrian's gaze fixed on me. Instead of returning to my seat, I scoot onto the couch beside him.

The lavender in his irises flares, an unearthly glow emanating from deep within. He takes the tea and sips it, his eyes regarding me over the cup's rim.

I turn to face him, folding my legs in front of me so my toes graze his thigh. I could be imagining things, but I swear he shudders at the contact. Could what I feel for these supernatural men be two-sided? Are they as irresistibly attracted to me as I am to them?

Elrian clears his throat and sets the cup of tea on the table. "If I wasn't clear earlier, I wanted to be sure you understood my intentions."

I swallow hard, the intensity of his gaze making it hard to breathe. "Okay…"

He takes my hand and gently brushes his thumb across my

palm. “I haven’t spent much time with humans—a fact that I’m beginning to regret. Life at Winter Court doesn’t allow for much frivolity. You’re not at all what I expected. I find myself inexplicably drawn to you, and I would like to stay in hopes of getting better acquainted.”

My skin tingles at his touch, and I find myself wanting his hands all over me. *Whoa there, Kimmie. Let’s rein in sultry vixen.* “I want that too,” I breathe.

“Good.” Releasing my hand, he shoots up before I can blink. “I’ll let you get some rest now.” He’s at the door so quickly I barely have time to answer.

“Okay, thanks for stopping by,” I call out as he practically sprints down the hall. With a quick nod to the big guy standing guard by my door, I turn the lock and trudge over to my bed. The small fire that Elrian had started fizzles away into frustration.

I’m never going to figure out the prince of the Fae.

CHAPTER 29

Methyss stands in front of me, his cheshire-cat grin taking up more than half of his face. Behind him on the raised platform stand all fifteen remaining bachelors. Agitated butterflies swarm to life in my belly. *I hate this part.*

Tipping his hat so that it sits just above his unruly brows, Methyss whispers, "Are you ready, Ms. Starr?"

My brain screams no, but I nod anyway, forcing my head to bob up and down.

"And we're rolling!" A sharp voice jerks my attention toward the camera operator—not Cross.

Methyss spins toward the camera and sweeps his hands out with a grand gesture. "Welcome, bachelors, to the night you've all been waiting for. I'm Methyss, your host for the evening and you all know the star of the show, Ms. Kimmie-Jayne Starr!" He motions to me, and I plaster on my best smile. A trickle of sweat snakes down my back, disappearing into the pitch-black of my curve-hugging dress. I'm suddenly very thankful Bash chose that color for today's elimination. It's the perfect hue to hide sweat stains.

"I would hope you all know her a bit better by now." A mischievous smirk lights up his orangey skin, and he winks exaggeratedly. A small wave of chuckles breaks through the crowd of men and heat crawls up my neck, staining my cheeks.

One of the guys catcalls, and I repress the urge to hide behind Obsidian's gilded cage. *Boys*! I scan the lot of them to figure out who the culprit is, but it's no use. They're all smiling like little angels now.

"Does everyone remember the rules?" Methyss addresses the bachelors. "If you receive a gold infinity pin move to the right, silver cupid pin to the left, and black skull and cross-bones—I'm afraid you move directly out the doors. No funny business, gentlemen. And now, without further ado, let the elimination begin!" Methyss nods to me and I open Obsidian's cage, allowing the creepy bird to perch on my arm.

I whisper a name into the crow's ear and watch as he alights on the table, carefully picking up a gold infinity pin. Starting on a positive note makes this whole terrible process slightly easier.

Obi flaps his ginormous wings and circles over the group of men, taking his dear sweet time. I clasp my hands together holding my breath. *Just do it already, stupid bird*!

The fact that today's elimination ceremony will also reveal the big supernatural twist has my insides contorting into giant pretzel knots. How will they do it? When will it happen? I just want this whole thing to be over already.

Finally, Obi lands on Fenix's shoulder, and I release the breath I've been holding as the bird drops the pin into his open palm. With a triumphant snicker thrown at his twin, he leaps off the platform, barreling over a few guys to reach me. He wraps me in his strong arms, clasping me by the back of the neck so I have no choice but to nuzzle into his chest. His warm smoky scent rolls over me, instantly transporting me back to our night in the cave. My pulse accelerates at the steamy memories and heat floods my cheeks.

Fenix leans down and whispers into my ear. "Thanks for sticking with me, treasure—even after finding out... everything."

I get up on my tiptoes and brush my lips against his stubbly cheek. "I should be thanking you for saving my life," I murmur.

"Okay, you two." Methyss attempts to step between us, but I'm reluctant to let go. "Save it for after the ceremony."

With a grumble, Fenix releases me and walks to the right side of the room. I immediately feel the absence of his warmth and goose bumps prickle my skin. I can't dwell on it long because Obi lands on the table and squawks. *Bossy bird*! He cocks his head at me, his little black beady eyes assessing... and I swear, judging.

I lean down and whisper another name, and he gets back to work. As I watch him, it suddenly occurs to me this is no normal bird. With all the supes running around here it only makes sense he would be one too.

Fraser lets out a "Whoop!" and a second later, the big Scotsman has me in his embrace. "Thank ye, lass. I hoped ye would pick me. I'm sorry we haven't had much of a chance to speak after—*our date*."

I almost forgot Fraser had been skydiving with us too. What in the world was he—the Loch Ness monster? Whatever he is, I want to know more about the dashing highlander. "I look forward to finding out more about you too," I finally say, and he happily turns off to join Fenix along the right wall.

The next two don't go as well. Klaus and Gunnar are both sent home, and I can't even meet their eyes as they trudge out of the room. The slam of the front door has a depressing ring of finality to it. Both men were there for me when the unicorn head appeared in my bathroom, but since then I hadn't really been able to connect with either. My shoulders sag, weighed down by my heavy heart as I whisper the next name to Obi.

Eli, Logan and Aren all get the silver cupids, and though none of them are thrilled on missing out on the gold pins, they take it in stride. I want to know more about these guys before I can commit. I can't shake the feeling that Aren had something to do with my miraculous stop at the edge of the cliff. There was something supernatural about the wind that halted us before my horse and I could tumble over.

I give them all warm smiles and hugs before they move to the left side of the room.

Flare shoots me a pout from across the way, and I decide to put an end to his suffering. I know the idea of his twin getting chosen before him has to be driving the proud dragon mad.

Obi drops a golden pin into his hand and by the time I blink, fiery green eyes are no more than an inch away. And then he erases the distance between us, his lips searing into mine.

The whole room explodes into thundering groans as Flare dips me backward and deepens the kiss. My toes curl as the big dragon's heat consumes me.

"Come on, Methyss! Keep Flare in line," shouts Cillian from the platform. His voice snaps me back to the present, and I wriggle out of Flare's heated embrace.

"Totally worth it," he mutters with a wink as he heads to the right to join his twin—his *intensely scowling* twin.

I shake my head, but I can't help the giggle that bubbles out. What am I going to do with those two? I block out the little voice in my head that asks how will I ever choose between the brothers…

Cillian's sky-blue gaze meets mine, and a smile instantly

appears on my face. My other protector. Giving him the infinity pin isn't even a question. I never feel safer than when I am with Cillian. With a word to Obi, he's off to deliver the next golden token.

Just a few more to go. I throw my shoulders back and prepare for the next eliminations. Nix and Easton both get the dreaded skull and crossbones. Easton is just too shy and never opened up to me. As for Nix, our interactions were limited and I didn't quite feel the spark.

Lucíano is next, my sexy Latin lover that I almost lost. Getting so close to losing someone forever has a way of bonding you in a manner that's not easily broken. As he approaches, slinking toward me like a panther, my core clenches. He presses his lips to my hand then kisses both of my cheeks.

"Thank you, amor. I am honored to be chosen yet again."

There's something about Lucíano that makes me think he's older than what he looks. The way he speaks, his old-school chivalry, it speaks of a different time. Maybe whatever he is allows him not to age. Or be killed... The thought lances through my mind, and I gasp. I quickly clap my hand over my mouth, but it's too late. Lucíano notices my reaction.

Could Lucíano have died and come back to life? Is he immortal?

"What's the matter, amor?" He squeezes my hands firmly between his.

"No-nothing," I stutter.

He gives me a tight-lipped smile and moves to the right wall to join the other gold-pinned bachelors. I watch him walk away as my mind spins. *This is what I signed up for,* I remind myself. So what if Lucíano is immortal, right?

I glance over at the table and cringe. Two cupids and one skull and crossbones remain.

Methyss appears beside me and places a hand on my shoulder. A tuft of orange hair spills out from underneath his top hat. "Are you ready for the final three choices, Ms. Starr?"

I gulp. *No*. I force myself to nod anyway.

I'm a chicken so I save the worst for last. The aloof Fae prince gets the cupid pin because despite his enigmatic personality, I can't help wanting him. His face is a perfect mask of calm when he approaches and takes my hand. Dropping a cordial kiss, his eyes finally meet mine.

"I'm pleased to continue this journey with you." Though he says the words, I can't help but notice a flicker of disappointment as he pins the silver token to his lapel.

"Me too," I mutter, and he walks off to join the others.

Obi drops the remaining cupid pin into Colt's hand, and he shoots me an indulgent smile. The sweet cowboy won me over on our group date to the waterfall before everything went to hell. Besides that, I really want to know what kind of supernatural becomes a veterinarian.

Obsidian perches on my arm as I stare across the way at the last remaining bachelor. I whisper to the crow as anxiety swirls in my gut. The second he's up in the air, my eyes cast down to the floor.

Loud cursing jerks my attention from the speckled marble to the angry bachelor. Ryder. Fiery yellow bursts flash across his pitch-black eyes as he glares at me from the raised dais. Eliminating him was one of the hardest decisions I'd made so far. I can't deny my attraction to him, and yet I wasn't able to get close enough to the bad boy to really get to know him.

Speaking of the bad boy—that side is flaring to life this very moment. He's equal parts captivating and scary as hell. His tattooed arms twitch, the corded muscles straining just below the surface. He's shooting daggers at me with those volatile irises. Whatever supernatural he is, he's a dark and powerful one.

Methyss moves between us, cutting me off from Ryder's black gaze. "Control yourself, Mr. Strong."

I peek around Methyss' lithe form to get a better look. Ryder squeezes his eyes shut and clenches his fists at his sides. When he reopens them, the yellow is gone, leaving only the bottomless black.

"This is a mistake," he grumbles as he stomps off the platform and out the door.

My heart twists painfully. I hate this. I hate hurting these men. For what—a TV show?

Methyss exhales a drawn out breath. "Well that's it, gentlemen. Congratulations, you've all made it to the next round." Then a devilish grin sneaks across the man's face. "Or have you?"

My eyes widen. *Oh fudge, here comes the twist.*

Methyss spins to me, his face aglow in orange, the lights bouncing off his bright white teeth. "I'm afraid you have one more decision to make, Ms. Starr."

I glance over at the ten remaining men lined up along the same wall now and wring my hands. "Okay…" I mutter.

"You see, Ms. Starr, there's something you don't know about all of these men. Something the majority of the world doesn't know. There's nothing ordinary about the ten remaining bachelors. They have all been keeping a big secret from you."

Cillian catches my eye and mouths, "Sorry," and my chest tightens. The air thickens, and it's hard to breathe. I want to scream for someone to just say it already. Get on with it!

I nod and attempt to keep my expression blank, reminding myself I have to pretend the big supernatural reveal is a surprise.

"Once they divulge this secret, you have a choice to make."

My eyes shoot up to Methyss's. "A choice?"

"I don't want to give it away too soon. What say we hear from the men first?" He claps his hands and all the lights extinguish, bathing the room in inky black. My heart jumps up my throat, and I bite my tongue to keep from screaming. A second later, a bright light explodes in the middle of the room. Only it's not a light—it's a shimmering orb, suspended in mid-air.

"You see, Ms. Starr, things are not always as they seem on reality television." Methyss waves his hand toward the bachelors, lighting up their dark forms and my jaw drops.

CHAPTER 30

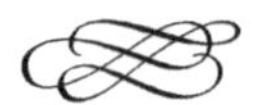

The two monstrous dragons—one gold and the other emerald green are the first to catch my eye. Then beside them stand what I can only guess is a gargoyle? The silver-winged creature is made of stone and wears a fierce expression, similar to ones I've seen perched atop churches. Next to the strange creature is Eli, only not quite—his bottom half has morphed into a neon blue fish tail. And Cillian—the most beautiful white wings have sprouted from his back. Rounding out the freaky creature show is a huge black wolf. He's the most normal of the bunch.

And Shep was worried that I wouldn't be able to pull off surprised? I don't think I'll ever be able to scrape my jaw off the floor. My hand is clasped over my chest as I stare unblinking at the pack of supes. Of the bachelors I do recognize—Elrian, Fraser, Lucíano and Aren, I'm scared to find out what secrets they're human-looking forms are hiding. Well, except for Elrian, which I already know are pointy ears and Fae princeliness.

When I finally pry the words out from the back of my

throat, my voice is a couple decibels higher than normal. "What in the world is going on?"

Methyss wraps his arm around my shoulder, his fine silk suit smooth against my bare back. "I'm afraid you've stepped out of the human world and joined us here in the supernatural one."

I nod, forcing my lungs to pump oxygen in and out.

He snaps his fingers and gilded signs appear across the chests of each of the bachelors. In glittery golden writing, letters begin to form.

My eyes scan over what I now realize are magical nametags.

Fenix – Dragon Shifter
Flare – Dragon Shifter
Logan – Gargoyle
Elijah – Merman
Cillian – Angel
Colt – Shapeshifter
Elrian – Fae
Lucíano – Vampire
Aren – Elemental Wielder
Fraser – Time Traveler

ONCE I READ each nametag twice, I suck in a breath. The edges of my vision darken, and my knees begin to wobble. Knowing supernaturals exist and seeing them in their actual forms are two completely different things. As the last week flashes through my mind, images of my interactions with these men flood my vision.

I got down and dirty with an angel?

Lucíano is a vampire...

Gargoyles and mermaids really exist?

I'm not sure how much more my poor human brain can take.

As if reading my thoughts—which he very well could be—I'm certain Methyss isn't human either, he turns to me. "I know this is a lot to take in, and you must have many questions. I'm sure the bachelors will be happy to answer them for you, but right now, you have another decision to make."

I groan. I'm not sure my brain is in a state to make any sort of decision.

A door opens and ten more guys walk in, lining up at the opposite side of the room. My jaw unhinges for the tenth time tonight as I ogle the troupe of handsome men.

Methyss points to the new arrivals and grins wickedly. "Ms. Starr, the choice is yours—knowing what you now do, will you continue the game with the ten supernatural bachelors you've chosen or would you like to replace them with these ten *human* men?"

Seriously? *This* is the other twist?

My eyes bounce back and forth between my guys and the new ones. I'm not going to lie; the new ones are definitely good looking. Unwittingly, I find myself searching for Cross among the humans. *Stupid—I know*. My gaze returns to the ten supes I've spent the last two weeks with, and my insides turn to goo. Does it really matter what they are? I've grown to care for each and every one of them in some way. I shouldn't let their paranormal status sway me. Right?

And yet, I could possibly marry one of these men. Can I really spend my life with a shifter, an angel or a *vampire*?

"Tick-tock, Ms. Starr," says Methyss. "I'm going to need an answer."

I snag my lower lip between my teeth and glance back and forth between the groups of guys. The two massive dragons' eyes sear into me, sending a wave of heat over every inch of me.

Aw, what the hell…

"I choose my guys—I choose the supernaturals."

The room explodes into whoops and cheers, and the huge knot in my gut begins to unravel. Before I can say another word, I'm engulfed in a sea of bulky arms and firm chests—and dragons and other unearthly creatures.

Methyss takes my arm, pulling me free from their enthusiastic embraces and twirls me toward the camera. "Very well, Ms. Starr. Your decision has been made. Wave goodbye to your would-be suitors."

I do as I'm told, and for the moment I'm happy in my choice. Even though someone is possibly trying to kill me, I'm sure my guys will protect me. I may not understand much about the paranormal world or what it means to be a merman or a gargoyle, but I know in my heart I'll be safe with them.

"Now what?" I ask Methyss.

"Now it's time for the celebration." He waves his hand and the back walls fall away, revealing a decadent ballroom. Lowering his head to my ear, he whispers, "You'll find things will become much more entertaining now that the truth is out." He winks. "Why be normal when you can have all of this?"

And just like that, we're back at the fantasy ball from the very first night. Only now I know that no one is in costume—the lithe figures flying overhead are fairies, the half-men half-beasts are shifters, and the mermaids in the pool are exactly what they seem.

Magic ripples around me; I can almost feel it in the air as Methyss escorts me inside the ballroom. The music vibrates the floor, and my body longs for a release. After all the pent up tension, I don't want to think anymore. I don't want to worry about being killed, about what the next few weeks will be like with a house full of supernatural men I'm totally crushing on. I just want to have fun.

As if they'd read my mind, Fenix and Flare appear, back in their fully male forms. "May we cut in?"

Methyss nods and releases my arm. "Enjoy your evening, Ms. Starr." He dips his head and disappears into the crowd.

Fenix inches closer and cups my cheek. "Are you all right?"

"I am." And for once I actually mean it. I place my hand over his and lean into his warm palm. "I probably have no idea what I'm getting into, but I'm glad I'll have you both along for the ride." Smiling at the handsome dragon twins, I know I made the right decision. I've never experienced anything close to the attraction I feel for them or the others.

"Okay, let go of her." Flare slaps his brother's hand away. "It's my turn." He takes my hand and leads me to the center of the dance floor. It doesn't take long for the other eight bachelors to join us. Within minutes, a champagne glass appears in my fingertips while my other fist pumps to the music.

The pulsating beat takes over my body and I let loose, dancing without a care. The guys encircle me, each taking turns wowing me with their dance moves. I can't help but laugh at some of their ridiculous efforts, but it's fun and freeing and I never want it to stop.

Five glasses of champagne later, Flare leads me back to my room. One arm is wrapped tightly around my waist, the other is carrying my stilettos. I've got a bad case of the giggles as we creep down the quiet hallway. I clap my hand over my mouth to keep them from bubbling out.

"I'm glad someone had fun tonight." Flare's warm breath

tickles my ear, and goose bumps prickle all the way down my arm.

"So much fun." I stop half way down the hall and push the big dragon up against the wall. He stills, his green-eyed gaze raking over me. I rise to my tiptoes, but he still has to bend to meet my lips. His mouth captures mine, warm and fiery much like the man I've pinned to the wall.

Boldly pressing my body into his, I let out a small moan. He swallows it up, deepening the kiss as my hands roam his sculpted back. He hitches his hand under my knee, and a second later my legs are wrapped around his waist like a koala. He spins us around, trapping me against the wall. I suck in a breath as his lips move down my neck.

"Maybe we should take this into my room," I rasp out.

A deep growl reverberates in his throat, and I take that as a yes. With long strides, he eats up the last few yards down the hall as I cling onto his broad shoulders.

He opens the door and his body tenses, a sharp hiss escaping his lips.

"What?" I struggle to rotate in his arms, but he keeps me pressed to his torso.

A slew of curses explode from his mouth, and my heart begins to race.

"What is it, Flare? Put me down. I need to see."

His big hand cradles the back of my head, keeping it firmly against his body. "No. You don't need to see this." There's a tremor in his voice that tells me I definitely do, even if I'm terrified.

"It's my room, Flare," I shout and leap out of his arms.

Big mistake.

The second my eyes scan my room, I wish I could take it all back. Deep red blood paints the walls, splattering in every direction. My gaze falls to the bed—to the crumpled body soaked in crimson liquid.

"Oh God, no." I clasp my hand over my mouth to keep from screaming. I can't see much through the bloody gore, but a blonde ponytail catches my eye. I step forward, but Flare's big arm comes around my waist.

"No, don't Kimmie. You don't want to see that close up."

"I have to." I force his arm off me and tiptoe toward the bed, warm blood squishing through my toes. *Oh stars, this just happened.* Nausea crawls up my throat, but I swallow it down. Whoever it is, is dead because of me.

Reaching the bed, I focus on the man's blood-spattered face. The blonde ponytail catches my eye once again, and I'm sure of it. It's Aren. The sweet, kind, funny bachelor who I'm fairly certain used his magic to save my life that day on the cliff.

My knees wobble as all the air siphons out of my lungs. *Oh no, oh no.* Ice ripples through my veins, panic's chilly fingers taking hold of me. The corners of my vision blur, and blackness seeps in. I take a step back, and my legs betray me. I wait for the smack of my body against the floor, but it never comes. Instead, a pair of warm arms weave around me as the darkness consumes me.

Book Two, Hitched: The Top Ten is out now and FREE in Kindle Unlimited! Read on for a sneak peek and a full list of the bachelors and their supernatural identities :) And don't forget to join GK's Supe Squad to vote for your favorite bachelor!

SNEAK PEEK OF HITCHED: THE TOP TEN

Chapter 1

I race down the spiral staircase, the black smoke billowing all around me so dense that my eyes water. My lungs struggle to suck in air amidst the suffocating smoke, but I force my legs to keep moving regardless. Where is everyone? I search the black for Faustus, Auriela, the guys, anyone—the manor is empty. Did they already get out?

A tremor shudders the ground beneath my feet, and I stumble over the last step and land in a heap in the middle of the grand foyer. The floor vibrates beneath the plush carpeting I luckily landed on. I tighten the tie around my robe and take a minute to catch my breath before pushing myself back up. Big. Mistake. I suck in a mouthful of smoke and cough like crazy, hot fiery pokers stabbing my lungs.

I leap toward the entryway and whip the double doors open, scrambling to get away from the choking black air. The moment I'm out, I gulp in a big breath only to discover columns of smoke wrapping like tendrils across the lawn. The grass is charred, and the beautiful angel fountain has been reduced to marble rubble. It looks like a war zone.

Half-men-half-animal creatures battle just outside the wrought iron gate encircling the compound. The clash of their weapons and guttural howls reverberate across my eardrums, and all I want to do is run back into the house. But I can't. The heat from the fire trapped inside nips at my shoulder blades. I must keep moving.

Sprinting down the steps, a spine-tingling shriek pierces the early-dawn sky. My eyes shoot up to a massive golden dragon sailing overhead.

Fenix!

An emerald green one darts up beside him, and the pair circle over the manor grounds.

Fenix? Flare? I reach out to them mentally like Fenix had when he saved me from plummeting to my death after my parachute malfunctioned on our skydiving date. *What's going on*?

Nothing. *Fenix? Flare*? I try again to no avail.

Staring up into the murky sky, more shadowy forms take shape. The unicorns! A herd of rainbow-winged horses gallop over my head with bow-and-arrow wielding riders.

What in the world?

A volley of white-flamed projectiles flies toward my boys, and I hold my breath. I wish I'd asked Fenix more about what can and can't kill dragons.

Dragon-Fenix and Dragon-Flare dip and soar dodging the blazing arrows and weaving in between their attackers. More dragons of every color suddenly appear on the horizon, and they dart into the fray. Their enormous bodies dwarf the unicorns but the flying horses are more nimble and easily evade the dragons' fiery breath and sharp talons.

A few errant flaming arrows land atop the manor setting

another corner of the roof ablaze. *So that's where the fire came from.* Another blood-curdling screech sends my gaze whipping up to the sky. An arrow protrudes from Dragon-Flare's chest, and he's falling fast.

No. My chest tightens as I watch helplessly as the enormous emerald dragon plummets to the ground, the earth trembling beneath my feet on impact. Steadying myself, I race across the driveway to the tennis courts where Dragon-Flare lies unmoving. The battle rages on above my head, but I don't dare look up. Sliding to my knees, I hover beside the enormous creature's head. His mouth is open, tongue hanging out and he's panting heavily. I ignore the sharp teeth and run my hand over his snout. He closes his eyes and makes a low huffing sound.

"Are you okay?" I whisper as my gaze runs down his body.

A glistening arrow made of a metal I've never seen sticks out of his chest, moving up and down with his haggard breaths. His scaly skin is covered with deep cuts and burns—how long has he been fighting?

"Flare, can you hear me?"

His eyes flutter open. The green of his irises is a ghostly reflection of its normal deep emerald hue. He huffs again but doesn't answer me.

Dark blood oozes from the arrow wound, a strange shimmery liquid mixed through it and quickly pools beneath his body. Are these arrows poisoned? I need to do something, but I have no idea what.

"How can I help you, Flare? Please, tell me what to do." I encircle my arms around his thick neck and press my cheek against his rough skin as tears fill my eyes.

A sharp crack reverberates across the sky, loud enough to drown out the surrounding sounds of battle and I crane my neck up once more. The clouds part, and a fissure splits the dark blue in two. From within the break in the atmosphere, a troupe of angels spew forth.

Cillian? At this distance, their faces are a blur, nothing but figures with sprawling wings joining the fray. If it is Cillian, then maybe he can heal Flare. Isn't that what angels do? A twinge of hope unfurls in my chest.

The big dragon chuffs, and I turn my gaze back to him. "Hold on, Flare. I'm going to get help." I leap to my feet and wave my hands in the air, jumping up and down. "Cillian! Help!"

More winged-human-figures approach from the east, but unlike the angels' feathery white wings, these appendages are half the size and nearly transparent. They too carry an assortment of weapons and now the four distinct groups engage each other in battle.

Oh my stars!

Focusing my eyes above, I search for Cillian's broad shoulders and golden hair. Somehow I know he has to be up there. Even squinting, it's no use. They're too far, and I can't make out clear details.

A blazing sword slices through the air, striking one of the unicorns. The animal rears up on its hindquarters and expels its rider. My breath catches in my throat as the body plunges toward the earth.

"Help him!" I cry out to no one. Why won't anyone help me?

Another man on unicorn dives to reach his falling comrade, but a dragon swoops down blocking his path. He's going to hit the ground. The realization freezes the blood in my veins as I run toward the spa—the body's apparent trajectory.

The figure hits a tree, sliding through the top branches and lands with a sickening thud on the burnt grass below. I reach him seconds later. As I creep closer, nausea claws up my throat. Wisps of platinum blonde hair cover a familiar face.

Elrian.

I sink to the ground beside him, focusing only on his porcelain skin. I don't want to concentrate on the unnatural contortion of his body. If I close my eyes a little, I can pretend he's only sleeping. I lift a shaky hand to his face and stroke his cool cheek. My shoulders shudder, and a sob builds in my tightening throat. Tears stream down my face as I caress the Fae prince I never really got to know.

All around me the battle rages on—the clang of swords and ferocious beastly growls only yards away. My feet are planted to the spot, not wanting to leave Elrian, but a part of me wants —no needs—to check on Flare. There's nothing I can do for the Fae prince now, but maybe there's still hope for my dragon.

Lowering my head, I brush my lips against Elrian's. A chill has already swept through his body and now invades my own. "I'm sorry," I whisper before running away.

Darting back to the front of the manor, the stabbing pain in my chest lessens at the sight of the enormous dragon. The end of the arrow bobs up and down slowly, confirming a haggard breath, but a breath nonetheless. I collapse down beside him and stroke his pointy snout. "Flare, I'm here. Please, tell me how I can help you."

His lids open, the green impossibly pale as he regards me with eyes of a man, not an animal.

You have to choose, Kimmie-Jayne. It's the only way to put an end to this. His faint voice tickles my mind, and I'm half certain I only imagined his words.

"What do you mean?"

His eyelids droop closed, and his words echo in my brain. *Kimmie, you have to choose. Kimmie...*

~

"Kimmie! Kimmie, wake up!"

Flare's deep voice draws me back from the brink of darkness. Like a lost ship at sea I follow the rough timbre of his voice to shore. My eyes snap open, and I jolt straight up.

"Flare! You're okay." I wrap my arms around his neck and pull him in tight. There's no war waging around us—in fact, the house is silent. Too silent. I glance around and recognize the pink walls of my room. I spin to the left, but Flare stops me.

"No. Don't look."

The blood. Aren. Dead in my bed. All the ghastly images come speeding across my mind on fast-forward. Bile creeps up my throat, and I think I'm going to be sick. I gag, and a second later Flare has me in the bathroom leaning over the sink. He holds my hair back as I wretch again and again. Though he doesn't say a word, his presence is soothing; his heat radiates through his shirt as he hovers behind me.

Finally, when there's nothing left but my hollowed out stomach, I rinse my mouth with some water, splash a bit on my face, and then straighten.

Flare's emerald gaze catches my eye through the mirror. "Are you okay?"

I shake my head. The battle had only been a dream, but this reality is nearly as bad. "Is that Aren out there?"

He nods, his lips pressed in a tight line.

My knees wobble, but Flare's there to catch me. I lean into his chest as his arms wrap around my waist to steady me.

"Stay in here. I'm going to get help." He lowers me onto the toilet seat and brushes his lips against my forehead.

I resist the urge to cry out for him to stay. I don't want to be alone with that ghastly scene only a few feet away in my bedroom. He turns toward the door, and I bite my tongue to keep from stopping him. "Just close the door, please," I mutter. At this angle, I can see the blood dripping off the corner of my bed.

Flare marches out of the bathroom, gently closing the door behind him and I wrap my arms around my torso to keep from falling apart. I only hope I can hold the pieces together until he gets back.

Chapter 2

A rush of voices seeps through the cracks in the door—muffled gasps and curses coming from my favorite executive team. Two light knocks resonate on the wood. I draw in a breath. "Come in."

Dax fills the doorway, his deep lavender hair hanging over his eyes. "Oh, sweetheart, are you all right?"

I fiddle with the hem of my black gown and shake my head, refusing to meet his gaze. I can't. I don't want to cry again.

Flare pushes his way by the director and crouches down beside me. Gently rubbing circles along my bare back, he whispers soothingly.

I can't believe this is happening. Shep had promised the *accidents* would stop once the big reveal was over. It hadn't. If anything, things were escalating.

Speak of the devil.

Sheppard and Tycen appear in the doorway, neither wearing their signature expensive suit. If I wasn't so upset about Aren, I might have said something about their abnormally casual attire.

"Are you okay?" asks Sheppard. For once, something like emotion flashes across his typically cold gray eyes.

I cock my head. "What do you think?"

He steps further inside the bathroom and leans against the countertop. I almost warn him to be careful for puke splatter, but I just don't care at this point. "I'm very sorry that you had to see that." He clasps his hands together, and it's the first glance of vulnerability I've ever seen in the man.

"Not as sorry as Aren." The words tumble out of my mouth before I can stop them.

Tycen looks horrified, and I don't blame him. It was a horrible thing to say. I fold over and bury my face in my hands.

"We need to ask you some questions," continues Shep.

Flare cuts him off with a growl. "You can't be serious. She's been through enough—just give her a second to recover. She passed out for gods' sakes."

How long was I out for? The dream seemed so real, but it could have only been a few minutes. As rattled as I am about Aren, I can't shake the disturbing images from the dream either.

Anger ignites from the hollowness in my gut, and I glare at Shep, Tycen and Dax. "You guys said we'd be safe. You said that once the truth was out, everything would stop." If we'd only suspended production, Aren would still be alive right now.

At least Sheppard has the decency to look ashamed for once. "I know. It pains me to say that I was wrong. I never thought that whoever is behind this would go to such lengths to keep us from airing."

"Why? Why would they?" None of this makes any sense to me.

Shep's expression darkens, and the blank mask he usually wears slides back on. "I don't know."

Liar!

I grunt and rake a shaky hand through my hair to smooth out the thick tangles. "If you don't need anything else from me,

I'd like to be alone." I need a shower, bad. If only the hot water could wash away the ickiness seeping into my pores.

Sheppard nods. "The police will be here shortly. I'm sure they will want to ask you some questions."

"Right."

Sam, Dax's assistant appears and weaves her way past the execs to me. "Come on, hun. Let's get you out of here."

Flare helps me to my feet and I follow Sam, making sure to shoot Shep and Tycen scowls on my way out. Dax's gaze is glued to the floor so he misses out on my disdain.

Flare takes my left side, his bulky frame blocking the gruesome scene on the bed. A part of me wants to look back—to get once last glance at sweet Aren, but I suppress the urge. I don't want to remember him that way. As it is, I doubt I'll ever get the ghastly image out of my mind.

Numbly, I trail behind Sam toward my old bedroom. Flare's arm is tight around my waist, his big body lending me strength. She opens the double doors to the master suite, and I never thought I'd be happy to be back here. The fake—or not fake—unicorn head pales in comparison to the horror in my former bedroom.

"Do you need anything?" Sam asks. Her usual no-nonsense look is miles away. I think she actually feels sorry for me.

"You got a valium?" I'm only half kidding. I'm exhausted, but I'm fairly certain sleep will not come easily tonight.

She clicks on the headset wrapped around her neck. "I can see what I can do."

I shake my head when she starts whispering into the speaker. "Nah, forget it. I'll settle for some of Auriela's herbal tea if you got it."

"That I know I can do." She spins toward the door. "I'll be right back," she calls over her shoulder.

I let out a sigh, and Flare leads me toward the ginormous

canopied bed. I'd forgotten how beautiful it was. He pulls out a corner of the comforter and motions for me to get in. I'm torn between exhaustion and the desire for a hot shower.

My body weighs a ton, dragged down by the mix of sadness and anger swirling through me.

"Come on, firecracker." He tugs me onto the bed. "You don't have to sleep if you don't want to, but you should at least sit down and rest."

"Okay." I crawl in, the mattress sinking beneath me like a heavenly marshmallow. I glance up at the anxious emerald eyes regarding me, and my heart swells. "Flare, I had the most terrible nightmare when I passed out. You were dying—or at least your dragon was, and Elrian was dead. There was a huge battle going on right on top of the manor with all these crazy supernatural creatures. Fenix was there and Cillian too. It was the most bizarre thing."

His dark brows furrow, his lips straightening into a tight line. "That does sound strange. I'm not surprised though with what you'd just seen." He leans closer and sweeps a strand of hair off my forehead and trails his fingers down my temple. "Just rest now, Kimmie. Everything will be better when you wake."

"Will you stay with me?"

"Of course." He sits down beside me just as Sam reappears with a mug of tea.

She hands it to me with a small smile. "Auriela says this will put you to sleep in no time."

My fingers curl around the cup, and its warmth seeps into my chilly palms. Taking a sip, I swirl the jasmine and apple-blossom fragrances around my mouth. My eyelids begin to droop and I wonder if this is some sort of magical concoction, but right now I'm too tired to care.

A few sips later, I fall into a deep, dreamless sleep.

~

A feather-light touch skims across my cheek, and my eyes flutter open. A part of me is annoyed by the disturbance, but the other half can't deny the flicker of heat the gentle caress elicits.

Sky-blue eyes hover over me and I start, surprised by the absence of the green I'd been expecting. "Cillian?"

"How do you feel, angel?"

I suppose I should be asking him the same thing. With everything that's happened, I haven't had a second to process all the guys' supernaturalness. And here sitting right beside me is an honest to goodness angel. An angel I am tempted to do very naughty things with. I push the wayward thoughts aside and focus on Cillian's worried expression.

"I'm okay, I guess." I glance at the clock on my nightstand. I only slept for a few hours. "Where's Flare?"

"He's talking to the detectives so he asked me to sit with you. I'm sorry to wake you, but it's your turn."

Ugh. Anxiety unfurls in my gut like a churning tornado, and I pull the covers up over my head. Talking to the police about what happened will make it real, and I'm not ready for that.

Cillian tugs at the comforter, and I peer over the edge of the soft linen. "I'm sorry, Kimmie, but you have to."

"I know. I know." I shove the sheets back and run my hand through my hair with a sigh. "Do I have a sec to take a shower?" I'm still wearing my fancy ball gown, and I'd rather not face the police in the over-the-top attire.

Cillian shoots me a smile. "I'll see if I can stall them if you promise to be quick."

"Deal." I jump out of bed and scurry into the bathroom. Stripping out of my black dress, I can't believe all that has happened in the past twenty-four hours. First, I discover the supernatural identities of each of the men I'm kind of falling for, then I lose one of those men and see my first dead body, then the freakishly weird dream, and now I'm about to be interviewed by the police about a murder.

How did this become my life?

A few weeks ago, all I cared about was finding an acting job and not being late to work at Pollo Loco. I step into the shower, and the sultry warm water pelts my skin. I wish it could wash away everything bad that's happened in the last few days. No such luck.

Continue reading Hitched: The Top Ten now! Join G.K. DeRosa's VIP Squad to get a freebie novella, special sneak peeks, bonus features, giveaways and more in a bi-monthly newsletter.

BACHELOR LIST

Top 15 Bachelors

- Fenix – Dragon Shifter
- Flare – Dragon Shifter
- Logan – Gargoyle
- Elijah – Merman
- Cillian – Angel
- Colt – Shapeshifter
- Elrian – Fae
- Lucíano – Vampire
- Aren – Elemental Wielder
- Fraser – Time Traveler
- Gunnar - Hunter
- Nix – Demigod
- Easton - Ghost
- Ryder - Demon
- Klaus - Werewolf

Don't forget to join GK's Facebook group, the Supe Squad to vote for your favorite bachelor and get a glimpse of the Top Ten!

ALSO BY G.K. DEROSA

ACKNOWLEDGMENTS

A huge and wholehearted thank you to my dedicated readers! I could not do this without you. I love hearing from you and your enthusiasm for the characters and story. You are the best!

A special thank you to my loving and supportive husband who always understood my need for escaping into a good book (or TV show!). He inspires me to try harder and push further every day. And of course my mother who is the guiding force behind everything I do and made me everything I am today. Without her, I literally could not write—because she's also my part-time babysitter! To my father who will always live on in my dreams. And finally, my son, Alexander, who brings an unimaginable amount of joy and adventure to my life everyday.

A big thank you to my new talented graphic designer, Sanja Gombar, for creating a beautiful book cover. A special thank you to my dedicated beta readers/fellow authors Jena, Kristin and Tiea who have been my sounding board on everything from cover ideas, blurbs, and story details. And all of my beta readers who gave me great ideas, caught spelling errors, and were all around amazing.

Thank you to all my family and friends (especially you, Robin Wiley!) and new indie author friends who let me bounce ideas off of them and listened to my struggles as an author and self-publisher. I appreciate it more than you all will ever know.

G.K.

ABOUT THE AUTHOR

USA Today Bestselling Author, G.K. De Rosa has always had a passion for all things fantasy and romance. Growing up, she loved to read, devouring books in a single sitting. She attended Catholic school where reading and writing were an intense part of the curriculum, and she credits her amazing teachers for instilling in her a love of storytelling. As an adult, her favorite books were always young adult novels, and she remains a self-proclaimed fifteen year-old at heart. When she's not reading, writing or watching way too many TV shows, she's traveling and eating around the world with her family. G.K. DeRosa currently lives in South Florida with her real life Prince Charming, their son and fur baby, Nico, the German shepherd.

www.gkderosa.com
gkderosa@wilderbook.com

CPSIA information can be obtained
at www.ICGtesting.com
Printed in the USA
LVHW111624130120
643458LV00001B/209/P